THE
ORANGE
GIRL

Also by Jostein Gaarder

Sophie's World
The Christmas Mystery
Hello? Is Anybody There?
The Solitaire Mystery
Through a Glass, Darkly
Vita Brevis
The Frog Castle
Maya
The Ringmaster's Daughter

THE
ORANGE
GIRL

Jostein Gaarder

Translated by James Anderson

Weidenfeld & Nicolson
London

A PHOENIX HOUSE BOOK

First published in Great Britain in 2004

A Phoenix House Book

© Jostein Gaarder 2003

Translation © James Anderson 2004

A CIP catalogue record for this book is available
from the British Library

ISBN 0 297 84904 2

Typeset by Deltatype Ltd, Birkenhead, Merseyside

Printed in Great Britain by Clays Ltd, St Ives plc

Phoenix House
Weidenfeld & Nicolson
The Orion Publishing Group Ltd
Orion House
5 Upper St Martin's Lane
London WC2H 9EA

www.orionbooks.co.uk

You can read about the Hubble Space Telescope at
http://hubblesite.org

My dad died eleven years ago. I was only four then. I never thought I'd hear from him again, but now we're writing a book together.

These are the very first lines of this book, and I'm the one doing the writing, but my dad will get his chance a bit later. He is the one with most to tell.

I'm not sure how well I remember my dad. I suppose I only think I remember him because I've looked at all the photos of him so often.

The only thing I'm really sure I can remember is something that happened when we were sitting out on the patio looking at the stars.

In one of the photos I'm sitting next to Dad in the yellow leather sofa in the living room. It looks as if he's saying something nice to me. We've still got that sofa, but Dad no longer sits in it.

In another picture we've settled down in the green rocking-chair in the conservatory. That picture has hung out here ever since Dad died. I'm sitting in the green rocking-chair now. I'm trying not to rock because I'm writing in a large exercise book. Later on, I'll enter it all on to Dad's old computer.

There's a tale to tell about the old computer, too, but I'll come back to that later.

It's always been strange having all these old pictures around. They belong to a different time from now.

In my room I've got an entire album of photos of Dad. It feels rather weird to have so many images of a person who's no longer alive. We've got Dad on video too. I think it's a bit scary listening to his voice. My dad had a really deep voice.

Maybe watching videos of people who aren't here any more, or who've passed on as Grandma puts it, should be made illegal. It doesn't feel right to spy on the dead.

I can also hear my own voice on some of the videos. It's squeaky and high-pitched. It reminds me of a little chick.

That was how it was in those days: Dad was the bass and I was the treble.

In one of those videos I'm perched on my dad's shoulders trying to snatch the star from the top of the Christmas tree. I'm not much more than a year old, but I very nearly manage to yank it off.

When Mum's watching videos of Dad and me, she'll sometimes sit back and laugh out loud, even though she was the one who held the video camera and did the filming. I don't think she should laugh when she watches videos of Dad. I don't think he'd have been happy about that. Perhaps he'd have said that it was breaking the rules.

In another video Dad and I are sitting in the Easter sunshine outside our cabin at Fjellstølen with half an orange each. I'm trying to suck the juice from my half without peeling it. Dad's mind is possibly on some very different oranges; in fact I'm pretty sure it is.

It was shortly after that Easter that Dad was taken ill. He was ill for more than six months and was frightened he was going to die. I think he knew he was going to die.

Mum has often said that what upset Dad more than anything was that he might die before he managed to get to know me properly. Grandma said something similar, only in a more mysterious way.

My grandmother's voice always takes on an odd tone when she talks to me about Dad. I suppose that's not so strange. Grandma and Grandpa lost a grown-up son. I don't know what that feels like. Luckily, they still have another son who's alive. But Grandma never laughs when she looks at the old pictures of Dad. She stays quite solemn. Those are her own words.

Dad had sort of decided that it wasn't possible to have a proper talk with a boy of three and a half. I understand why he thought that now, and you, the reader, soon will as well.

I've got a photo of Dad lying in a hospital bed. His face is very thin in that picture. I'm sitting on his knees while he grasps my hands to prevent me falling on top of him. He's trying to smile at me. This was just a few weeks before he died. I wish I didn't have that picture, but because I have got it, I can't throw it out. I can't even stop myself looking at it.

I'm fifteen now, or fifteen years and three weeks to be precise. My name is Georg Røed and I live in Humleveien – 'Bumblebee Road' – in Oslo together with my mum, Jørgen and Miriam. Jørgen is my step-dad, but I just call him Jørgen. Miriam is my baby sister. She's only eighteen months old and much too young to talk to properly.

Obviously there aren't any old pictures or videos of Miriam and my dad. Jørgen is Miriam's father. I was Dad's only child.

There will be some interesting revelations about Jørgen right at the end of this book. They can't be divulged yet, but if you read on you'll find out.

After Dad died, Grandma and Grandpa came here and helped Mum sort through all his stuff. But there was one important thing that none of them found. It was a long story Dad had written before he was admitted to hospital.

At the time no one knew that Dad had written anything. The story of 'The Orange Girl' only turned up on Monday. Grandma had been into the tool shed, and there she found a complete story tucked in the lining of the red push-chair I'd sat in when I was little.

Just how it got there is a bit of a mystery. It can't have been totally accidental, because the story Dad wrote when I was three and a half had connections with that push-chair. I don't mean it's a story about a push-chair, it isn't, but Dad had written the whole of that long story for me. He wrote the story of 'The Orange Girl' so that I could read it when I was old enough to understand it. He wrote a letter to the future.

If it really was Dad who stuffed all the pages of that story into the lining of the old push-chair, he must have had a lot of faith in the notion that post always gets there in the end. It's occurred to me that for safety's sake it's a good idea to examine all old items carefully before giving them to a jumble sale or simply chucking them into a skip. I can't imagine how many old letters and suchlike might be found in a rubbish tip.

This is something I've thought about quite a lot over the past few days. I think there should be a much simpler way of

4

sending a letter to the future than cramming it into the lining of a pram.

Occasionally we want someone to read what we have written in four hours', fourteen days' or forty years' time. The story of 'The Orange Girl' was just that. It was written to the twelve- or fourteen-year-old Georg, a boy my dad hadn't yet met, and who perhaps he'd never live to know.

But now it's about time my story had a proper beginning.

A little under a week ago I got home from my music lesson to find Grandpa and Grandma had paid us a surprise visit. They had suddenly driven up from Tønsberg and were staying until the following morning.

Mum and Jørgen were there too, and all four of them sat looking eagerly expectant as I came into the lobby and began to kick off my outdoor shoes. My shoes were wet and muddy, but nobody took any notice. They had something else on their minds. I could feel it in the air.

Mum said that Miriam was in bed, and that seemed right somehow because Grandma and Grandpa were there. Well, they're not Miriam's grandparents. Miriam has her own Grandma and Grandpa. They're nice people too, and sometimes they come to see us, but people do say that blood is thicker than water.

I went into the living room and sat down on the carpet, while everyone looked so solemn that I thought something serious had happened. I couldn't remember doing anything wrong at school during the past few days, I'd got back home from my piano lesson at the normal time, and it had been months since I'd last taken a ten-kroner coin from the kitchen sideboard. So I said. 'Has something happened?'

At this Grandma began to describe how they'd found a letter Dad had written to me just before he died. I felt the pit of my stomach heave. I wasn't even sure if I could remember him. A letter from Dad sounded really formal, almost like a will.

I noticed that Grandma had a large envelope in her lap, and now she handed it to me. It was sealed and on the outside all that was written was 'To Georg'. It wasn't Grandma's handwriting, or Mum's, or Jørgen's either. I ripped open the envelope and pulled out a thick wad of paper. What a shock I had when I read the first line:

Are you sitting comfortably, Georg? It's important that you're at least sitting tight, because I'm about to tell you a nailbiting story . . .

My head was reeling. What on earth *was* this? A letter from my dad. But was it genuine?

'Are you sitting comfortably, Georg?' I thought I could hear the deep rumble of his voice, and now not just on video; I heard my father's voice as if he'd suddenly come alive again and was sitting in the room with us.

Even though the envelope had been sealed when I opened it, I had to ask the grown-ups if they'd already read the long letter, but they all shook their heads and said they hadn't read a word.

'Not a syllable,' said Jørgen. He sounded a bit bashful, and that wasn't exactly his style. But perhaps they'd be allowed to read Dad's letter after I'd finished, he suggested. I think he was very keen to know what was in the letter. I sensed that he had a guilty conscience about something.

Grandma explained why they'd jumped into the car and driven to Oslo that afternoon. It was because she believed she might have solved a long-standing puzzle, she said. This sounded pretty mysterious, and it was.

When my dad was ill he told Mum that he was in the process of writing something to me. It was a letter I was to read when I got older. But no such letter had ever come to light and now I was fifteen.

What had happened now was that Grandma had suddenly remembered something else Dad had talked about. He had insisted that no one should take it into their heads to throw out the red push-chair. Grandma thought she could recall his exact words as he lay in hospital. 'Don't ever get rid of the red push-chair, will you?' he'd said. 'Don't, please. It's meant such a lot to Georg and me these last few months. I want Georg to have that push-chair. Tell him that sometime. Tell him, when he's old enough to understand, that I really wanted to take care of it for him.'

And so the old push-chair was never thrown out or given to a jumble sale. Even Jørgen got instructions about it. Ever since he moved into Humleveien he'd known there was one thing he wasn't allowed to touch, and that was the red push-chair. In fact he showed such respect for it that he insisted on buying a brand new push-chair for Miriam. Perhaps he didn't like the idea of wheeling his own daughter around in the same push-chair that my dad had walked me in many years ago. But it's also possible that he wanted a newer and trendier push-chair. He's quite fashion-conscious, not to mention affected.

So, there was a letter and a push-chair. But it took Grandma eleven years to crack this puzzle. It had only just dawned on her that someone might go out to the tool shed and take a closer look at the old push-chair. And Grandma's suspicions were fully justified. The push-chair wasn't just a push-chair. It was a letterbox.

I wasn't quite sure if I believed this story. It's never possible to tell if parents and grandparents are telling the truth, at least not when 'sensitive issues' as Grandma calls them, are at stake.

Looking back now, I think the biggest riddle of all was why nobody had the sense to get Dad's old computer working eleven years ago. That was what he'd written the letter on! They'd tried to get it going of course, but they hadn't got the imagination to guess his password. It was a maximum of eight letters – that's what computers were like in those days. But even Mum never managed to break the code. It's unbelievable. So they simply dumped the computer up in the attic!

But Dad's PC is something I'll return to.

Now it's about time to hear from Dad. But I'll be slipping in a few comments of my own along the way. I'll also add a postscript. I need to do this because, in the course of this letter, Dad asks me a serious question. It makes a lot of difference to him how I answer it.

I got a Coke and took the letter into my room. When, for once in my life, I locked my door from the inside, Mum made a fuss, but she knew it was no good.

Reading a letter from someone who's no longer alive seemed so special that I couldn't bear the thought of all my relatives tiptoeing round me. It was a letter from my own father after all, and he'd been dead for eleven years. I needed a bit of peace.

It was strange holding those many pages of printout in my hands. It felt a bit like discovering a completely unopened photo album with brand new pictures of Dad and me. Outside it was snowing hard. It had begun to snow while I was on my way home from my music class. I didn't think the snow would lie. It was early November.

I lay on my bed and began to read.

Are you sitting comfortably, Georg? It's important that you're at least sitting tight, because I'm about to tell you a nailbiting story. Maybe you're already stretched out comfortably in the yellow leather sofa. Though I know nothing any more – you may have changed it for a new sofa. But I can just as easily imagine you've settled in the old rocking-chair in the conservatory, the one you were always so fond of. Or are you out on the patio? I don't know what time of year it is. And then, perhaps you don't even live in Humleveien now.

What do I know?

I know nothing. Who is the Prime Minister? What is the name of the Secretary-General of the UN? And by the way, how is the Hubble Space Telescope doing? Do you know? Have the astronomers found out any more about how our universe is put together?

Several times I've tried to think myself into the future, but I've never got close to conjuring up a proper image of you as you are now. All I know is who you used to be. I don't even know how old you are as you read this. Maybe you are twelve or fourteen and I, your father, have long since made my exit from time.

The truth is that I feel like a ghost already, and I have to catch my breath each time I think about it. I begin to understand why ghosts go in for so much sighing and hooting. It's not to scare their descendants. It's just that they find it so hard to breathe in a time other than their own.

We don't only have a place in existence. We also have an allotted span.

That's the way things are, and all I can do is extrapolate from what's around me now. I'm writing in

9

August 1990.

Now – I mean as you read this – you'll certainly have forgotten most of what we both enjoyed together during these warm summer months when you were three and a half. But the days are still ours, and we still have many fine moments ahead of us.

I'll tell you something that occupies my thoughts a lot at the moment: each day that passes, and each small thing we find to do together, increases the chance that you'll remember me. I count the weeks and days now. On Sunday we went up the Tryvannstårnet observation tower and looked across half the kingdom; we saw all the way to Sweden. Mummy, too, all three of us were there. But can you remember that?

Could you just try, Georg? Please, just try, because everything is stored up inside you somewhere.

Do you remember your big wooden train set? You play with it for hours every day. I glance down at it now. At the time of writing, trains, track and ferries lie strewn across the lobby floor, just as you left them a short while ago. In the end I just had to haul you away from it so that we'd get to assembly at the nursery school on time. But it's as if your small hands are still moving the pieces. I haven't dared shift so much as a piece of rail.

Can you remember the computer that you and I play games on at the weekends? When it was very new, it lived up in my study, but last week I moved it down to the lobby. Now I only want to be where all your things are. And, of course, in the afternoons you and Mummy are here as well. Grandma and Grandpa visit more often, too. And that's good.

Do you remember your green tricycle? It's almost

brand new and is parked out on the gravel drive. If you haven't forgotten it, that's probably because it's still somewhere in the garage or tool shed, old and worn out, I dare say. Or did it end up at a jumble sale?

And what about the red push-chair, Georg? Yes, what of *that*?

You must at least have some memories of all the walks we had round Lake Sognsvann? Or from all our visits to the cabin. We've been to Fjellstølen three weekends in a row. But I don't dare ask any more now, quite literally, because perhaps you just can't recall anything from that Georg-time that was also my time. I have to accept things are they are.

I said I was going to tell you a story, but it's not so easy to find the right tone for this letter. I've probably already made the mistake of addressing the little mite I feel I know so well. But you're no longer a small boy as you read these lines. You're no longer the little lad with the golden curls.

I can hear myself prattling on, the way elderly ladies baby-talk to toddlers, and that's silly, because it's the grown-up Georg I'm trying to reach – the one I never managed to see, the one I never managed to have a proper talk to.

I look at the clock. It's only an hour since I got home after taking you to nursery school.

Whenever we cross the stream, you always have to get out of your push-chair and throw a stick or a stone into the water. The other day you found an empty bottle, and so you threw that as well. I didn't lift a finger to stop you. You're allowed to get away with rather a lot

11

nowadays. And when we arrive at nursery school, you often rush straight inside before we've managed to say 'see you' to each other. It's as if you're the one with no time and not me. It's an odd thought. Old people often seem to have more time than small children with their entire lives ahead of them.

As for me, I'm no age to boast of; I consider myself to be a young man still, a young father in any event. And yet, more than anything else, I'd like to halt time. I wouldn't mind one day lasting for ever. Evening and night would come of course, for the day has its own pattern, its own revolving rhythm, but then the following day could start just where the previous one did.

I no longer feel the need to see and sense more than I've already experienced. I just want so desperately to hang on to what I have. But there are thieves about, Georg. Unbidden guests have started sucking the vital force out of me. They should be ashamed of themselves.

It feels specially good and particularly hard to take you to nursery school at the moment. Even though I still have no problems moving about, or even pushing you in your push-chair, I know that my body is seriously diseased.

It's the harmless illnesses that make the patient bedridden immediately. A serious disease usually requires a longer time to flatten you for good. Perhaps you won't remember that I was a doctor, although your mother must have talked a bit about me, in fact I'm sure she has. Although I've got leave from my job at the group practice, I know what I'm talking about. I'm no gullible patient.

And so there are two periods in this reckoning of ours, or in this very last meeting between the two of us. It almost feels as if we're each standing on our own misty mountain top trying to spy each other. Between us lies an enchanted valley that you have just put behind you on your journey through life, but which I shall never live to see you in. Even so, I must try to relate both to these mornings when you're at nursery school – the time of writing – and to the time of reading, which will be yours alone, when you sit down with this.

I should tell you that it makes me feel deeply emotional writing this letter to a bereaved son, and it must hurt a bit to read, too. But you are a little man now. If I've managed to commit these lines to paper, you must bear to read them.

As you realise, I've faced up to the fact that I'm possibly about to go away from all this, from sun and moon and all existence, though most of all from your mother and you. It's the truth, and it hurts.

I must put a serious question to you, Georg, and that's why I'm writing. But to be able to pose this question I must first tell the nailbiting story I promised you.

As long as you've been alive, I've longed to tell you about the Orange Girl some time. Today – I mean at the time of writing – you're much too young to understand the story. And so it must form my small bequest to you. It will have to lie waiting for another day in your life.

Now that day has come.

When I'd read this far, I had to look up. I'd tried to remember my dad lots of times, and now I tried again. He'd asked me to. But all I seemed able to see was images from the videos and the photo album.

I remembered having a large wooden train set when I

was young, but that didn't help me remember Dad. The green tricycle still lived in the garage, and so I was fairly sure I could recall that from my childhood as well. And the red push-chair had always lived at the back of the tool shed. But I couldn't bring back any of the trips round Lake Sognsvann. Nor could I remember going up the Tryvann-stårnet observation tower with Dad either. I'd been to the observation tower lots of times, but that was with Mum and Jørgen. Once I'd been there alone with Jørgen. It was while Mum was in hospital after having Miriam.

Of course I had tons of memories from the cabin at Fjellstølen, but there wasn't room for Dad in any of them. There was only Mum, Jørgen and baby Miriam. We have an old guest book in the cabin and I've often read what my dad wrote in it before he died. The problem was simply that I didn't know if I could remember anything he was writing about. It was roughly the same as with all the photos and videos. 'On Easter Saturday Georg and I built a record-breaking igloo complete with snow lanterns . . .' Of course I'd read all these entries, and knew some of them by heart. But I'd never managed to remember being part of the event described. I was just two and a half when Dad and I built that record-breaking igloo with all its snow lanterns. We've got a picture of it too, but it's so dark all you can see is the candles.

Then there was something else that my dad had asked about in that long letter I'd only just started to read:

And by the way, how is the Hubble Space Telescope doing? Do you know? Have the astronomers found out any more about how our universe is put together?

Reading this sent a shiver down my spine, because I'd just

recently completed a large special assignment on the Hubble Space Telescope. Other people in my class had written about British football, the Spice Girls or Roald Dahl. But I'd gone to the library and brought back everything I could find on the Hubble Space Telescope and written my special assignment on that. I'd handed it in to my teacher only a few weeks ago, and in the file I'd produced he'd written that he was very impressed with 'such an adult, thoughtful and well-informed approach to a difficult subject'. I don't think I've ever felt so proud as when I read that sentence. As a headline to his comments the teacher had written, 'Laurels for an amateur astronomer!' And he'd also drawn a crown of laurels as well.

Could Dad be clairvoyant? Or was it pure coincidence that he was asking me about the Hubble Space Telescope only a few weeks after I'd completed my special assignment?

Or wasn't the letter from Dad genuine? Or was he still alive? This sent another shiver down my spine.

I sat on my bed thinking hard. The Hubble Space Telescope had been put into orbit around the earth from the space shuttle Discovery on 25 April 1990. It was just around then that Dad became ill; he got sick just after the Easter holidays in 1990. I'd always known that, it was just that I hadn't clicked that it was at exactly the same time as the Hubble Space Telescope began to orbit the earth. Perhaps Dad found out that he was ill on the very day that Discovery was launched from Cape Canaveral with the Hubble Space Telescope aboard, perhaps in the same hour, the same minute.

If so, I could well understand why he was so preoccupied about the fate of the space telescope. In fact, they had quickly discovered that there was a serious problem with the optics of the telescope's main mirror. Dad couldn't know that this defect was repaired by astronauts from the space shuttle Endeavour in December 1993, as that was almost exactly three years after he died. Nor, of course, did he know about all the fantastic extra equipment that was added in February 1997.

Dad died before he could register that the Hubble Space Telescope's pictures of the universe were the clearest and best ever taken. I had found a lot of them on the internet and made a great pile of copies for my special assignment. Some of my favourites are also hanging up in my room, such as the crystal clear image of the giant star *Eta Carinae* which is more than 8,000 light years away from our own solar system. *Eta Carinae* is one of the most massive stars in the Milky Way and will soon explode into a supernova before finally imploding and forming a neutron star or a black hole. Another favourite is the picture of the huge gas and dust clouds in the Eagle Nebula (also known as M16). This is where new stars are born!

We know a lot more about the universe now than we did in 1990, largely thanks to the Hubble Space Telescope. It has taken thousands of pictures of galaxies and nebulas many millions of light years from the Milky Way. It has also taken some incredible pictures of the universe's past. It sounds a little daft to say that it's possible to take pictures of the universe's past, but looking out into the universe is the same thing as looking back in time. Light travels at a speed of 300,000 kilometres per second, but even so, light from distant galaxies can take billions of years to reach us because the universe is so incredibly vast. The Hubble Space Telescope has taken pictures of galaxies that are more than twelve billion light years away, but this also means that it has seen more than twelve billion years into the universe's past. This is mind-boggling, because at that time the universe was less than one billion years old. The Hubble Space Telescope has virtually managed to see right back to the Big Bang, when time and space were created. I know a little bit about this, and that's why I'm writing about it now. I must take care not to put down *everything* I know. The assignment I handed in to my teacher was forty-seven pages long!

I thought it was really weird that Dad was writing to me about the space telescope. I've always been interested in space research, and perhaps the ability to lift your gaze from the things happening around you on the surface of this planet can be inherited to some extent. But I could just as easily have chosen to do my special assignment on the Apollo programme and the first men on the moon. I could have written about galaxies and black holes too, not to mention galaxies *with* black holes. I could have written about the solar system with its nine planets and the great asteroid belt between Jupiter and Mars. Or I could have written about the huge telescopes on Hawaii. But I chose to write about the Hubble Space Telescope. How could Dad have guessed that?

It was easier to understand why he mentioned the UN Secretary-General. That was almost certainly because I was born on 24 October, UN Day. The name of the UN Secretary-General is Kofi Annan. And the Prime Minister of Norway is Kjell Magne Bondevik. He's just replaced Jens Stoltenberg.

While I sat there thinking, Mum knocked at the door and asked how it was going. 'Don't disturb me,' was all I said. I'd hardly read four pages.

I thought: Tell me, Dad, tell me about the Orange Girl. Here I am and the day has arrived. Now is the time for reading.

★

The story of the Orange Girl began one afternoon when I was standing outside the National Theatre waiting for a tram. It was sometime towards the end of the 1970s, and it was late autumn.

I remember I was thinking about the medical course I'd just begun. It was strange trying to imagine that one day I'd be a real doctor dealing with real patients who would come to me and place their destiny in my hands. I would be there in a white coat, sitting at a large desk saying: 'We'll do some blood tests, Mrs Johnsen.' Or: 'How long have you had this?'

Then finally the tram appeared. I could see it a long way off, as it glided past the Parliament building and then trundled slowly up Stortingsgaten. Something that has troubled me ever since is that I've never been able to recall where I was going. But in any case I was soon boarding the bright blue Frogner tram, and it was jam-packed with people.

The very first thing that caught my eye was a lovely girl who was standing in the aisle clutching a huge paper bag brimful of luscious-looking oranges. She was wearing an old, orange anorak, and I remember thinking that the bag she was holding was so large and heavy that she might drop it at any moment. But it wasn't really the bag of oranges that made the biggest impression on me, but the young woman herself. I realised immediately that there was something very special about her, something unaccountably magical and enchanting.

I also noted the way she looked at me and seemed to pick me out from all the other people who'd come swarming on to the tram – this only took a moment, it was almost as if the two of us already enjoyed some kind of clandestine alliance. As soon as I was inside, she fixed me with a level gaze, and perhaps I was the first to look away, it's quite possible, because I was uncommonly shy in those days. And yet, I recall thinking quite lucidly and clearly during that brief tram journey that this was a girl I would never forget. I didn't know her name or who she was, but right from that first moment she exercised an almost uncanny power over me.

She was half a head shorter than me and had long, dark hair, brown eyes and was somewhere in the region of my own age, nineteen. As she glanced up, seeming almost to nod at me without moving her head in the least, she sent me a teasing, mischievous smile, almost as if once, a long time ago, we'd shared a whole life together, just her and me. It was as if I was reading something of that sort in her brown eyes.

Her smile had enticed a couple of dimples out into her cheeks and, though it had nothing to do with them, she reminded me of a squirrel; she was certainly every bit as cute. If we really had spent a life together, perhaps it was as two squirrels in a tree, I thought, and the idea of living a playful squirrel's life with this mysterious orange girl was hardly uninviting.

But why was her smile so knowing and provocative? Was she really smiling at me? Or was she just smiling at some funny idea, something that had suddenly struck her and that had nothing to do with me? Or was she smiling *about* me? That, too, was a possibility I had to consider. But then, I wasn't especially amusing to look at, I thought I looked pretty normal, and it was she, not I, who had a decidedly comic air with that enormous bag of oranges pressed to her stomach. So perhaps that was why she was smiling – at herself. Perhaps she liked laughing at herself. Not everyone has that ability.

I didn't dare look her in the eyes again. I simply stared at the great bag of oranges. She'll drop it in a minute, I thought. She mustn't drop it. But drop it she did.

There must have been at least five kilos of oranges in that bag, maybe eight or ten.

The tram was making its way up Drammensveien. You must try to imagine it. It jolted and swayed, it stopped at the US Embassy, it stopped at Solli Plass, and then, just as it was about to turn up Frognerveien, what I'd been fearing all along, happened. Suddenly the Frogner tram listed dangerously − or at least that was what it felt like − the orange girl tottered slightly, and in that split second I knew that I must save the enormous bag of oranges from catastrophe. Now . . . no, now!

It was then that I made what was perhaps a fatal miscalculation. At any rate, I initiated a fateful course of action. Just listen to this: I resolutely stuck out both my arms and quickly had one hand under the brown paper bag and the other firmly round the waist of the young woman. What do you think happened next? Well, the girl in the orange anorak lost her bag of oranges of course, or rather I pushed them up out of her tight grasp, almost as if, mad with jealousy, I wanted to shove them out of the way. The deplorable result was that thirty or forty oranges were set rolling about, in people's laps, on the floor, well, just about all over the tram. I'd no doubt done lots of idiotic things before, but this took the biscuit; it was the most embarrassing moment of my entire life.

So much for the oranges at present. Let's leave them rolling about in the tram for a few seconds more, because this tram story isn't really about them. The girl was soon looking at me again, and now she wasn't smiling any more. At first she just looked upset, at least a dark shadow passed across her face. I couldn't tell what she was thinking, of course I couldn't, but it looked as if she was about to burst into tears at any moment. It was as if each orange had had a special significance for her, yes, Georg, as if each and every one of them was quite irreplaceable. This passed off quickly, because the next moment she was looking up at me with an annoyed expression, showing quite plainly that she held me responsible for what had happened. It felt as if I'd ruined her life, not to mention my own. It felt as if I'd wrecked my own future.

You should have been there at the time and defused the situation for me; you might have said something funny and disarming. But I had no small hand to hold at the time – it was many years before you were born.

Covered with shame, I got down on all fours and began to gather up oranges from amongst a forest of mucky boots and shoes, but I only managed to rescue a fraction of them. I soon discovered that the bag that once held them had burst and was now quite unusable.

It struck me as a bitter joke that I had – quite literally – fallen flat on my face for this young girl. A couple of passengers began to chuckle with amusement, but only the most good-natured among them, because there was no shortage of irritated looks as well, as the tram was very full and the crush almost unbearable. I noted that the passengers who'd seen what occurred regarded me as the culprit, when all I'd intended was a gallant rescue.

The last thing I recall from that ill-fated trip is the following image: I'm standing there with my arms full of oranges, I've stuffed two of them in my pockets as well, and just as I reappear before the girl in the orange anorak, she looks me right in the eye and says caustically: 'You twit!'

I'd been told off and no mistake, but then she reassumed some of her humour and said half mollified, half derisively: 'Can I have an orange to take with me?'

'Sorry,' was all I said. 'Sorry!'

Just then the tram pulled up at Møllhausen's café at Frogner, the doors opened, I nodded in confusion to what, in my eyes, was the almost supernatural orange girl, and the next moment she simply picked up one of the oranges from my precarious armful and vanished into the street as playfully as a sprite in a fairytale.

The tram gave another lurch and trundled on up Frognerveien.

'Can I have an orange to take with me?' Georg! But after all, they were her oranges I had in my arms, and my pockets, while the rest rolled around on the tram floor.

Now I was the one with an armful of oranges, and they weren't even mine. I felt like some mean orange thief – one or two of the passengers hinted at much the same thing through amused little comments – and I can't remember what went through my mind, but I crept out of the tram at the next stop, which was Frogner Plass.

As I got off the tram the only thought left in my head was to dump all the oranges somewhere. I had to teeter like a tightrope walker so as not to drop them, but even so one of them fell on to the pavement, and of course I couldn't risk stooping down to pick it up.

Shortly afterwards I caught sight of a woman pushing a pram past the old fish shop, you know, the one on Frogner Plass. (Well, it may not be there any more.) I approached the woman slowly and, just as I passed the pram, I took the opportunity to unload all the oranges on to a pink baby cover, even the ones in my pockets; it was the work of only a second or two.

You should have seen the look on that woman's face, Georg. I felt I had to say something, and so I asked her if she'd be kind enough to accept my small gift on behalf of the little baby as, with winter fast approaching, it was vital that children got enough vitamin C. It was something I knew about, I added, because I was a medical student.

No doubt she thought I was impertinent, perhaps she thought I was drunk, she certainly didn't believe I was studying medicine, but I was already running hell for leather down Frognerveien. Again I had only one idea in my head: I had to find the orange girl again. I had to trace her as fast as possible and make amends.

I don't know how well you're acquainted with that part of town, but I soon arrived breathless at the intersection of Frognerveien, Fredrik Strangs Gate, Elisenbergveien and Løvenskioldsgate, where the mysterious girl had got off the tram with a single, solitary orange in her hand. I might as well have been standing on the Place de l'Etoile in Paris, there were so many roads to choose from, and the orange girl had vanished.

I paced up and down Frogner for hours that afternoon. I went all the way up to the fire station at Briskeby, and right down to the old Red Cross Clinic, and every time I saw anything vaguely resembling an orange anorak, I felt my heart leap in my breast, but the girl I sought seemed to have evaporated.

Some hours later it struck me that the young woman I'd inconvenienced so thoroughly might have been ensconced safely at a window in Elisenbergveien, secretly watching a young student running up and down rather like the perplexed hero in the film version of an action-packed fairytale. He couldn't find the princess he was seeking. No effort was spared, but he was totally unable to track her down. It was as if the whole film had got caught in a loop.

At one point I saw some fresh orange peel in a rubbish bin. I picked it up and sniffed it, but if it really had belonged to the orange girl, it was the very last trace she'd left.

The rest of that evening I thought of nothing but the girl in the orange anorak. I'd lived in Oslo all my life, but I'd never seen her before, I was sure of that. It made me even more determined to do everything in my power to meet her again. As if by magic she'd already managed to interpose herself between me and the entire rest of the world.

Again and again I thought of all those oranges. What did she want with them? Was she literally going to peel each one in turn and eat them segment by segment for breakfast or lunch, for example? The thought inspired me. The thought that maybe she was ill and on some special diet also struck me and made me uneasy.

But there were other possibilities. Perhaps she was going to make orange mousse for a party with a guest-list of more than a hundred. The idea immediately made me jealous, for why hadn't I been invited to the party? I also had the notion that there might be a very uneven representation of the sexes at this party. Over ninety young men had been invited and only eight girls. I thought I knew why. The orange mousse was to be served at a large, end-of-semester bash at the Norwegian

School of Management, and because the subject was management there would be hardly any female students there.

I tried to banish the thought, it was unendurable, and I found it a scandalous disregard of equal opportunities that the School of Management hadn't yet adopted female quotas. Well no, my imagination was unreliable, of course. Perhaps the orange girl was simply on her way back to a cramped bedsit, there to squeeze litres and litres of orange juice so that she could store it in the fridge, either because she hated, or was allergic to, the juice the dairies manufactured from cheap Californian concentrate.

Neither juice nor mousse seemed especially likely. But soon I had a more convincing idea: the orange girl had been wearing an old anorak of the type Roald Amundsen had used on his famous polar journeys. I had always been good at reading signs – in medicine it's called diagnostics – and you don't go round the streets of Oslo in an old anorak unless it means something, at least not when you're lugging a huge bag full of juicy oranges about at the same time.

I arrived at the idea that the orange girl was clearly planning to ski across Greenland, or at least the Hardangervidda plateau, and naturally in that case it would be a good idea to have eight or ten kilos of oranges in the sled: without them she might risk dying of scurvy out in the wilds.

Yet again I let my imagination get the better of me, for wasn't 'anorak' an Eskimo word? Of course she was going to Greenland. But how would her Greenland expedition fare now? Did this mysterious girl have enough money to buy another load of oranges? She had practically burst into tears when she lost the whole of the big bagful, and I'd already concluded that she must be very poor.

But there were many variations. I had to come to my senses and see that. Maybe the orange girl was one of a large family. Well, why not? One couldn't just assume she was a nursing assistant living alone in a small bedsit opposite the Red Cross Clinic. Perhaps she might be one of the daughters in an extensive and orange-loving family. A family I would so like to have visited, Georg; I could imagine them round the large dining table in one of those fine old flats in the Frogner district with high, airy ceilings decorated with ornamental plasterwork. In addition to the mother and father there were seven children in the family, four sisters and two brothers excluding the orange girl herself. She was the eldest of the siblings, she was the loving and caring eldest sister. Qualities she would require to the full in the future, as now it might be many days before any of the little ones got an orange to take to school with them.

Or – and the thought ran like a cold shiver through my body – she could herself be the mother of a little family that consisted of her and a Mr Nice Guy who had just graduated from the School of Management, and their little four or five-month-old daughter, whose name I imagined, for some reason, must be Ranveig.

There was also another thing I had to regard as a possibility. It wasn't necessarily the mother herself who had been pushing the little baby beneath the pink baby cover outside Frogner Fish and Game. She might just have been the orange girl's nanny. The idea was painful, even though it would mean that some of the oranges found their way back to the young woman with the squirrel's gaze. The world had suddenly become so small, and there was a significance in everything.

I had always been particularly good at putting two and two together. I should add that I was the one who diagnosed my own illness when I knew I was sick. I'm rather proud of the fact. I simply went to a colleague and told him what was wrong with me. Then he took over. And afterwards . . .

Well, Georg, here I must take a little break from my writing.

Perhaps you find it strange that I've been able to write so jauntily about what happened that afternoon all those years ago. But I remember it as an amusing story, almost like a silent film, and that's how I want you to see it. This doesn't mean I'm especially light-hearted as I write. The truth is that I feel totally helpless, or totally inconsolable, to be more honest. I'm not trying to hide it, but it's something you're not to worry about. You'll never see my tears, I've made up my mind about that, and I'll manage to control myself.

Mum is on her way home from work, and we two are alone at home. But, just now, as you sit on the floor drawing with some coloured crayons, you cannot comfort me. Or maybe you can, after all. In years to come when you read this letter from the man who once was your father, maybe then you'll send him a consoling thought. The thought warms me already.

Time, Georg. What is time?

I glanced up at a picture of *Supernova 1987A*. The picture was taken by the Hubble Space Telescope at about the time Dad realised he was ill.

I felt sorry for him of course. But I wasn't sure I felt it was right for him to unload all his unhappiness on to me. I couldn't do anything for Dad. He lived in a different time from now, and I had my own life to lead. If everyone drowned in letters from dead fathers and forefathers, they would never be able to live their own lives.

I felt a couple of tears welling up in my eyes. They weren't sweet tears, if there's such a thing as sweet tears; they were those hard, cross tears that didn't flow but just sat burning in the corners of my eyes.

I began to think of all the times Mum and I had been to the cemetery and tended Dad's grave. After reading the last few paragraphs, I decided I wouldn't do that again. At any rate, I certainly would never set foot in the cemetery alone. Never.

It isn't necessarily hard to grow up without a father. It only gets really scary when a dead father begins to speak to you from the grave. Perhaps it might have been best if he'd left his son in peace. He'd even hinted at something about coming back as a ghost.

My palms were sweaty. But of course I would read the rest of Dad's letter. Maybe it was a good thing he'd written a letter to the future, and maybe not. It was much too soon to have any real opinion about it.

What a weirdo he must have been, I thought, at least when he was nineteen during that autumn at the end of the seventies, because he seemed to make such a big deal out of the way a girl was standing on the Frogner tram with a big bag of oranges in her arms. It's pretty normal for boys and girls to steal glances at each other. I imagine they've done that ever since the time of Adam and Eve.

Why couldn't he simply have written that he'd fallen in love with her? The girl must have realised that long before he attacked her oranges. He'd made sure one arm was round her waist as well. Perhaps he'd stood there on the tram with a subsconscious desire to do an orange-girl tango with her.

When children fall in love, they either start fighting or pulling each other's hair. Some chuck snowballs at each other, as well. I'd thought nineteen-year-olds would be a bit more sensible.

But I'd only read the opening of the story. Perhaps there really was something mysterious about this 'orange girl'. If not, Dad would hardly have begun telling a story about her. He was ill and knew he might die. So what he was writing about had to be very important to him, and perhaps to me too.

I drank the rest of my Coke and read on.

Would I ever meet the Orange Girl again? Perhaps not, perhaps she lived in a totally different part of the country, perhaps she'd only been in Oslo on a brief visit.

It became a habit, whenever I was in town and caught sight of a Frogner tram, to look in all the windows to see if the Orange Girl might be amongst the passengers. I did this lots of times, but I never saw her. I'd begun to take evening strolls in the Frogner area, and every time I caught sight of anything yellow or orange in the street, I thought now, now, I would meet her again! But though my expectations were high, my disappointments were many.

The days and weeks passed, and one Monday morning I dropped in to one of the cafés on Oslo's main thoroughfare, Karl Johan – it was a kind of meeting place for some of us students. No sooner had I pushed open the door and stepped inside, than I stopped short and staggered back a step or two. There was the Orange Girl! She'd never been there before, well, never at the same time as me, but now there she sat in the café with a teacup, flicking through a book of colourful illustrations. It was as if some invisible hand had placed her there in the expectation that I would drop in and pay her a visit. She was dressed in the same worn anorak, and listen to this, George – you may not believe this – but perched on her lap, wedged in between her and the small café table, was a huge paper bag full of succulent oranges.

I started. Seeing the Orange Girl again in the same orange anorak with an identical bag of oranges on her lap seemed as unreal as a mirage. From that moment on the oranges began to form the kernel of the truth I had to seek out. What kind of oranges were they, anyway? Their golden skins seemed to shine so brightly that I felt like rubbing my eyes. Their colour was of quite a different hue to the oranges I'd seen before. Even with the peel on I seemed to be able to smell their tanginess. Ordinary oranges they certainly were not!

I all but tiptoed into the place and seated myself at a table a few yards from her. Before I decided what course of action to take, I wanted just to sit and look at her, to enjoy the sight of the inexplicable.

I didn't think she'd noticed me, but all at once she glanced up from the book she was reading and looked me straight in the eyes. In doing this she caught me red-handed: now she realised that I'd been sitting there all the time observing her. She sent me a sunny smile, and what a smile, Georg; it was a smile that could have melted the whole world, because if the whole world had seen it, it would have had the power to stop all wars and hatred on the face of the planet, or at least there would have been some long ceasefires.

I no longer had any choice, I just had to go over to

her now. I crossed the floor slowly and sat down on a chair at her table. She didn't think it strange, although something in her demeanour made it hard to work out if she recognised me from the tram journey.

For several seconds we just sat there looking at each other without speaking. It was as if she didn't want us to begin talking right away. She looked into my eyes for a long while, for a whole minute at least, and this time I didn't look away. I noticed that her pupils were quivering. It was as if her eyes were asking: do you remember me? Or: don't you remember me?

One of us had to say something soon, but I was so flummoxed that I just sat there thinking of the time we'd lived together as a pair of playful squirrels in our own little spinney. She'd enjoyed hiding from me, I'd had to dart up and down the tree tunks trying to find her, and if I did catch sight of her she would merely leap from her branch over to another tree. And so I'd be forever frolicking after her through the trees, until one day I hit on the idea of hiding myself. Then she was the one who came mincing after me – I might be right up in the crown of a tree, or down in the moss behind an old stump, enjoying the sight of her searching impatiently for me, and perhaps her search was tinged with a pang of fear that she might never find me again . . .

Suddenly, something marvellous happened, not in the squirrel spinney back in the dawn of time, but there and then in a café on Karl Johan.

I had rested my left arm on the table, and now all at once she put her right hand in mine. She had placed her book on top of the bag of oranges which she still hugged with her other arm, almost as if she feared I might take it away from her or knock it to the floor.

31

I no longer felt so shy. I only sensed a cool power flowing out through her fingers and into mine. I thought that she possessed some kind of supernatural power, and I suspected that it was connected with the oranges in some way.

A riddle, I thought, a marvellous riddle!

I could no longer sit still without someone breaking the silence, and perhaps that was a betrayal, perhaps it was a contravention of the code the Orange Girl represented. We were still looking into one another's eyes when I gasped: 'You're a squirrel!'

When I had spoken, she gave a gossamer smile and squeezed my hand tenderly. Then she released it, rose majestically from the table with the great bag of oranges in her arms and tripped out into the street. As she went I saw she had tears in her eyes.

I was paralysed. I was speechless. Only a few seconds before the Orange Girl had been sitting opposite me holding my hand; the scent of oranges still seemed to linger in the room, but now she was gone. Perhaps, if it hadn't been for the bag of oranges, she might have waved. But she needed both arms to carry the large load so there was no opporunity for that. But she wept.

And I didn't follow her, Georg. That, too, would have been a breach of the rules. I was simply overwhelmed, I was exhausted, I was replete. I had experienced something delightfully mysterious that would keep me going for months. I'd certainly meet her again, I thought. There were powerful, but also inscrutable forces at work here.

She was a stranger. She came from a more beautiful fairytale than ours. But she'd managed to find her way into our reality, perhaps because she had an important mission here, perhaps because she was here to save us from what people sometimes call 'the monotony of life'. Until that moment I'd been completely ignorant of such missionary work. I'd thought there was only one existence and one reality. But there were two types of people at least. There was the Orange Girl, and there were the rest of us.

But why were her eyes filled with tears? Why was she crying?

I remember thinking that perhaps she was clairvoyant. Why else should she be moved to tears by the sight of a complete stranger? But perhaps she could 'see' that one day I would be brought low by an unkind fate.

It's odd to think that I could ever have imagined anything like that then. Although I've always been easily led by my imagination, I was, and I remain, a rational person.

At this point in my story I feel the need for a brief resumé. I promise this won't happen too often.

A young man and an equally innocent young woman exchange fleeting glances on a Frogner tram. They're no longer children, but they haven't reached full adulthood either, and they've never met before. Several minutes later, the young man thinks the young woman is about to drop a huge bag of juicy oranges. He leaps into action with the dismal result that all the oranges hit the deck. The young woman calls him a twit and gets off the tram at the next stop, asking only if she can take just one miserable orange with her, and in his confusion the young man nods. Several weeks go by and they meet again in a café. Once again the young woman is clutching a great paper bag full of lovely oranges. The young man moves to her table, and they sit like this for a full minute

33

looking into one another's eyes. This might sound a bit of a platitude, but during those sixty seconds they really do look deep into each other's eyes, almost to the bottom of each other's souls. She lays her hand in his hand and he says she's a squirrel. Then she rises gracefully and sails out of the café with the great bundle in her arms. The young man can see that she has tears in her eyes.

Only four lines have been spoken by these two. Her: 'You twit!' Her: 'Can I have an orange to take with me?' Him: 'Sorry, sorry!' And him: 'You're a squirrel!'

The rest is dumb-show. The rest is a riddle.

Can you solve this riddle, Georg? I couldn't, and maybe that was because I was a part of it.

Now I was well caught up in the story. Twice in a row the Orange Girl had appeared to Dad, each time with a big bag of oranges in her arms. It was mysterious. Then, without saying so much as a word, she'd taken his hand and looked deep into his eyes before jumping up suddenly and running weeping into the street. It was odd behaviour. It was singular.

Was Dad having hallucinations, or what!

Perhaps the Orange Girl was what they call a 'chimera'. Many people claim to have seen a sea monster in Loch Ness, or in Lake Seljordsvannet for that matter, and who can be certain they're lying? It may be they've seen a chimera. If Dad had suddenly started claiming that the Orange Girl had gone the length of Oslo's main shopping street hauling a huge dog sled, I'd be in no doubt that the story of the Orange Girl was really a product of how, for a short period of his life, he'd been on the point of losing his marbles. It can happen to the best of us, and there are things you can take for it.

Whether the Orange Girl was fanciful or flesh and blood, it was certainly clear that Dad had been terribly fixated on her. So, when he did get the chance to say something to her, I consider the sentence 'You're a squirrel' was a pretty hopeless line. He made no attempt to hide the fact that he was surprised at himself for saying something so clumsy. Why on earth had he said that? No, Dad, this is a riddle I don't know the answer to.

I'm not trying to be a know-all. I'd be the first to admit that it's not always easy to find something to say to a girl you 'like the look of', as they say.

I've already mentioned that I play the piano. I'm not exactly a super pianist, but I can manage the first movement of Beethoven's Moonlight Sonata almost without playing a false note. When I'm sitting alone playing the first movement of the Moonlight Sonata, I sometimes get the feeling I'm sitting on the surface of the moon playing away on a large grand piano as the moon and the piano and I sail round the earth. I imagine that the notes I'm playing can be heard all over the solar system, if not all the way to Pluto, then at least as far as Saturn.

I've just begun to practise the second movement of the Moonlight Sonata as well (*Allegretto*). It's a bit harder to get into, but it's really cool to listen to when my piano teacher plays it to me. It makes me think of little mechanical dolls running up and down the stairs of a shopping centre!

I've decided to drop the third movement of the Moonlight Sonata, and that's not just because it's too difficult, but also because I really find it scary to listen to. The first movement (*Adagio sostenuto*) is beautiful, and maybe a bit eerie, but the final movement (*Presto agitato*) is thoroughly menacing. If I was in a spaceship and landed on a planet where some sad creature was thumping out the

35

third movement of the Moonlight Sonata, I'd take off again immediately. But if it had been playing the first movement instead, I might have stayed there a few days, and I would at least have dared approach the creature to find out more about what things were like on the musical planet I'd come to.

I once said to my piano teacher that Beethoven had a lot of heaven and hell in him. Her mouth fell open at last. She said I was on the right track! Then she told me something interesting. It wasn't Beethoven who'd called it the Moonlight Sonata. He'd called it Sonata in C minor, Opus 27 number 2, adding that it was *Sonata quasi una Fantasia*, which just means 'a sonata like a fantasy'. My piano teacher thought the sonata was much too ominous to be called the Moonlight Sonata. She related that the Hungarian composer Franz Liszt had said that the second movement was like 'a flower between two precipices'. Personally, I would have called it 'a comic puppet show between two tragedies'.

But I was saying that I had no problem understanding the difficulty of knowing what to say to a girl you 'like the look of'. And now I'm going to make a real confessison, because in questions of that sort, I've already got my own skeletons in the cupboard, or at the music school, to be more precise.

Every Monday I have a piano lesson from six to seven in the evening. At the same time there's a girl who has a violin lesson; she's maybe a year or two younger than me, and she's someone I could sort of say I 'like the look of'. Quite often we sit in the waiting room together for five or ten minutes until our lessons begin. We've hardly said a word to each other, but a week or two ago she asked me what the time was, something she did again the following week. So I said that it was pouring cats and dogs outside and that her violin case had got wet. I have to admit that's as far as we've got. Because she doesn't start a proper conversation with me, I don't dare to launch into one with her, either. Perhaps she thinks I look like a geek. It's also possible that she likes me, but is just as shy as I am. I've no idea where she lives, but I know her name is Isabelle, because I've seen it on the list of violin pupils.

We've begun arriving earlier and earlier for our music classes. Last Monday we spent almost fifteen minutes waiting. But all we do is sit there. We don't say a word. Then we each go to our rooms and play for our teachers. Once or twice I've fantasised about her slipping into the piano room while I'm playing the Moonlight Sonata, and getting so caught up in that she begins to accompany me on her violin. It won't ever happen, it's just a figment of my imagination. Perhaps the reason I have this chimera is because I've never seen her violin. I've never heard her play it either. For all I know she may have nothing more inside her violin case than a recorder! (And then she wouldn't be called Isabelle. She'd just be called Anne.)

What I'm trying to say, I suppose, is that I have no idea how I'd react if she suddenly held my hand and looked me deep into the eyes. I don't know what I'd do if she began to cry, either. I realise I'm only four years younger than my dad was when he met the Orange Girl. I can understand how he went into a state of shock. 'You're a squirrel!' he said.

I think I know you pretty well, after all, Dad. Now, carry on with your story.

After that brief meeting in the café, my search for the Orange Girl began its systematic and logical phase, for again there were many long days when I didn't even catch a glimpse of her.

I'm not going to bore you with all my searches and

blind alleys, Georg; it would take too long anyway. But I cogitated and reasoned and one day I came to this conclusion: both times I'd seen the Orange Girl had been on a Monday. Why hadn't I thought of that before! Then there were the oranges – they were the only real clue I had to go on. Where did they come from? Oranges could be purchased in the Frogner shops, of course. Certainly they could, but how nice or juicy – or cheap – were those oranges? Someone who's really choosy buys oranges from a large fruit market, I thought, like the one at Youngstorget, which at the time was the only really big fruit and vegetable market in Oslo, at least for anyone who consumes several kilos of them a day. After a visit there, one might take the tram back to Frogner from Storgata, if one hadn't got the money to sit back in a taxi. But there was another clue too: the brown paper bag! An ordinary shop generally hands out plastic bags. But at Youngstorget fruit market weren't all the purchases packed into brown paper bags like the ones the Orange Girl had been carrying?

This was just one of many theories, but on three Mondays in a row I was to be found buying some fruit and vegetables in Youngstorget fruit market. A student's diet always left room for improvement, and recently I'd fallen into the habit of eating rather too much fast food.

I don't need to describe the teeming crowds at Youngstorget, Georg; all you need to do is follow my example. You're simply on the lookout for a mysterious anorak-clad girl at one of the stalls, haggling over the price of a ten-kilo bag of oranges – or trying to catch sight of the same young woman in the act of leaving the market with the heavy bag in her arms. You can forget everything else, everyone else, I mean.

But can you see her, Georg?

I was disappointed on the first two occasions I went there, but on the third Monday I caught sight of an orange figure at the far end of the market, and yes, what I was looking at was a young girl in an old anorak, and wasn't she standing at one of the fruit stalls filling a large paper bag with oranges?

I stole across the market and was soon standing just a few yards behind her. So this was where she bought them! It was like catching her in the act. I felt my knees knocking and I was frightened I was going to sink to the ground.

The Orange Girl still hadn't finished loading her bag with oranges, and the reason for that was that she had a way of buying them quite different from the other customers. Just listen to this: I stood for a long time watching the way she picked up the oranges one by one, assessing each one most critically before either placing it in the bag or back in the great bin it had come from. I could see why she didn't want to buy her oranges at any old shop in Frogner. This young woman needed a really huge selection of oranges to choose from.

I'd never seen such pickiness in selecting oranges before, and I suddenly felt certain that this girl didn't buy them simply to squeeze the juice out of them. But what then did she use them for? Have you any suggestions, Georg? Can you fathom out why she should spend nearly half a minute deciding whether to add this or that orange to her paper bag?

I had only one suggestion. The Orange Girl was in charge of the kitchen of a large nursery school where each child got an orange for elevenses. Now, it's a well-known fact that children have a very pronounced sense of fair-

39

ness. And so the Orange Girl's job was to make sure that all the oranges she bought were exactly the same; the same size, the same roundness, the same bright orange colour. She also had to count them.

I thought this was pretty convincing, and I even managed to feel a pang of anxiety over the fact that there might be several good-looking youths on the work-experience scheme at her nursery school. But, from a couple of yards away, Georg, I quickly ascertained that this was far from the case. It wasn't difficult to see that the Orange Girl made every effort to pick out oranges that were as different from one another as possible, in size, shape and colour. And here's a small detail for you: some of the oranges came with a leaf attached!

It was a relief to jettison the thought of those pushy work-experience types. But that was the only thing I could rejoice at. A riddle she was, and a riddle she remained.

The bag was filled, the Orange Girl paid the trader and began walking towards Storgata. I followed at a distance, because I'd made up my mind not to reveal myself until we were once again aboard the Frogner tram. But, sadly, on this crucial point I'd made a false assumption. She didn't walk all the way down to Storgata to take the tram this afternoon. Just before we arrived there, she got into a white car. It was a Toyota, and there was someone sitting in the front seat. It was a man.

I didn't exactly feel I could run up to her now. I wasn't all that keen on meeting the man. Soon the car pulled away, turned a corner and was gone.

But here is one important additional piece of information for you: just as the Orange Girl was getting into the car with the big bag in her arms, she sudddenly turned and looked at me, though whether she recognised me from the Frogner tram or the café on Karl Johan, I can't be certain. I'm only sure that she got into a white Toyota with a man and that she looked at me as she did so.

And who was this lucky man? I hadn't an opportunity to see how old he was; he might have been her father for all I could tell, but he might also be . . . but then, what did I know about it? Was he on work experience? In a white Toyota – hardly. Or was he that all-Norwegian clown of a father to a four-month-old girl called Ranveig? Not necessarily, nothing pointed to it. For that matter it was just as likely the Toyota man was the one the Orange Girl was going to ski across Greenland with. I had long since formed a picture of this man. In reams of images I could see the orange rations, the ice-axes, the first-aid equipment, the spare ski sticks, the sleeping bags, the primus stove and the Oxo cubes. I could see the tent they would live in, it was yellow, and I decided there were eight dogs in the team.

Naturally I could picture them! They mustn't run off with the idea that they could hide from me. It was as if I had a whole reel of film in my head: an odd couple skiing slowly across the miles of the Greenland ice-cap. She, as lovely and pure as the driven snow; but not him, he had a crooked nose, a bitter twist to his mouth and a gaze as deep with callous intent as the crevasses she might at any moment fall into. (Would he help her out of the crevasse? Or would he sprint off on his own to nourish himself on her orange ration in the full knowledge that he'd never meet her again?) He was possessed of a cruel, masculine force, a primitive and unlovely power. He shot polar bears with as little concern as others swat mosquitoes. And while we're on the subject, it had to be assumed that he was quite capable of raping her out there amongst the blocks of ice, far away from anything that could be called social justice. For who could see them now? Who could keep an eye on them out there? I tell you, Georg, it was only me. I was able to get a sharper and sharper picture of the whole expedition. I had full cognisance of all the equipment they had to take with them. Before the day was out, I had christened all the eight dogs, and during the evening I'd written out a list of supplies they had to take with them: altogether it weighed two hundred and forty kilos, including a small bottle of shampoo, and a quarter of a bottle of spirits they could drink when they arrived at Siorapaluk or Qaanaag . . .

By next morning my nerves had settled down. One doesn't traverse Greenland in December. In December such expeditions head for the Antarctic, and one would hardly buy oranges at a fruit market in Oslo, but make any necessary purchases in Chile or South Africa. It's not likely oranges would even be on the shopping list. Anyone going to the South Pole on skis must ingest so many calories per day that a special vitamin supplement would hardly be required. Anyway, oranges are too heavy a food, and most telling of all: how does one eat a frozen orange with hands encased in thick polar mitts? For raising the body's liquid levels on a polar expedition, oranges would prove about as inauspicious as Captain Scott's ponies. But then, there's liquid and liquid: one doesn't need more than a few drops of petrol and a good primus. Ice and snow – water in other words – is about the only thing there's plenty of in those regions, and over eighty per cent of an orange is water.

Dear, sweet little Orange Girl, I thought, who are you? Where do you come from? Where are you now?

Mum had come to the door again. 'How's it going, Georg?' she asked.

'Fine,' I said. 'So now you can stop fretting.'

She was silent for a second or two, then she said: 'I don't like you locking your door.'

'What's the point of having a key to a door if you don't use it now and then?' I said. 'There's such a thing as personal space, you know.'

This miffed her a bit. Or perhaps it's more correct to say it offended her. 'Now you're being childish, Georg. You've no reason to lock yourself away from us.'

'Yeah, right. I'm fifteen, Mother. I'm not the one being childish.'

She gave a big, peevish kind of sigh. Then all went quiet.

Naturally I didn't say anything about the Orange Girl. I had the strong feeling that everything Dad was telling me now was stuff he'd never mentioned to Mum. Otherwise *she'd* have been able to tell me about her, and Dad wouldn't have needed to spend his final days on earth writing me a long letter. Maybe he'd experienced something when he was young that he was now taking the opporunity to warn his son about, sort of man to man. He certainly had something important he wanted to ask me.

The most concrete thing he'd enquired about so far was how the Hubble Space Telescope was getting on. If only he'd known how much I could have told him about it.

The most 'special' thing about that 'special assignment'

was that our teacher had made me read it out to the class. I had to show the pictures as well. He meant well, but even during the next break some of the girls began to call me 'little Einstein'. They just happened to be the same girls who are dead keen to experiment with eye make-up and lipstick. I think they experiment with a lot more besides.

I've nothing against eye make-up and lipstick. But the fact is we're actually living on a planet in space. For me that's an extraordinary thought. It's mind-boggling just to think about the existence of space at all. But there are girls who can't see the universe for eye-liner. And there are probably boys whose eyes are never raised above the horizon because of football. There can be quite a chasm between a small make-up mirror and a proper mirror telescope! I think it's what they call a 'matter of perspective'. Perhaps it could also be called an 'eye-opener' as well. It's never too late to experience an eye-opener. But many people live their entire lives without realising that they're floating through empty space. There's too much going on down here. It's hard enough thinking about your looks.

We belong on this earth. I'm not trying to dispute it. We're part of nature's life on this planet. Monkeys and reptiles have shown us how we breed, and I have no quarrel with that. In different natural surroundings everything might have been very different, but here we are. And I repeat: I'm not denying it. I just don't think that prevents us from trying to see a little beyond the ends of our noses.

'Tele-scope' means something like looking at things far away. But could this story about an 'orange girl' really have anything to do with a space telescope?

The aim of siting a telescope in space was obviously not to get *closer* to the stars and planets the telescope was to study. That would have been about as daft as standing on tip-toe to get a better picture of the craters on the moon. The whole idea of a space telescope is to study space from a point outside the earth's atmosphere.

Lots of people think the stars twinkle in the sky, but in fact they don't. It's just our variable atmosphere that gives that impression, in roughly the same way the rippling surface of a lake can give the impression that the stones beneath are wavy and indistinct. Or the reverse: from the bottom of a swimming pool it's not easy to see what's happening above the surface.

There is no telescope on the earth's surface that can give really sharp pictures of space. Only the Hubble Space Telescope can. That's why it can tell us far more about what is out there than terrestrial telescopes.

Many people are so short-sighted that they can't tell a horse from a cow, or a hippopotamus from a zebra if you prefer. Such people need glasses to see better.

I wrote that a serious problem with the optics of the Hubble Space Telescope's main mirror was quickly detected and that the crew of Endeavour repaired the defect in December 1993. But they didn't actually do anything to the mirror itself. They just put glasses on it. These spectacles consist of ten small mirrors and are called COSTAR, or *Corrective Optics Space Telescope Axial Replacement*.

But still I couldn't fathom how the space telescope could be connected with the 'orange girl'. I understand now 'at the time of writing', but only because I read through the whole of the lengthy letter Dad wrote me in the weeks before he died. I've read it four times to be exact, but I won't divulge anything for new readers.

Just tell the story, Dad! Tell it to all those reading the book now.

The next time I saw the Orange Girl was on Christmas Eve; Christmas Eve, just imagine it! And this time I had a proper conversation with her. Well, we exchanged a few words, anyway.

At that period I shared a small flat in Adamstuen with a student friend called Gunnar. But I was to spend Christmas Eve at home in Humleveien with my family. There would only be Mum and Dad and my brother, your Uncle Einar. Einar, who's four years younger than me, was in his final year at secondary school that winter. This was years before Grandma and Grandpa moved to Tønsberg.

I had almost given up the idea of meeting the Orange Girl again, and I was also very unsure as to who the man in the white Toyota could be. Then I suddenly had the impulse to go to a Christmas service before heading home to Humleveien. So intoxicated was I by the mysterious girl that for some reason I conjectured that she, too, might attend a Christmas service before settling down with the people she was to spend Christmas with. (Who was it? Who were they?) I decided the cathedral was the most likely place to meet her, or the least unlikely to be more precise.

For the record, I need to make it clear that nothing I say about the Orange Girl is made up to enhance the story. Ghosts tell no lies, Georg, they have nothing to gain from it. But on the other hand, I'm not revealing everything either. Who has ever set out on such a futile

46

mission?

I can skip all the fruitless attempts I made to meet the
Orange Girl again. I spent days and weeks combing the
Frogner district, but I'm not going to describe it. If I did,
this would turn into a very lengthy and long-winded tale.
I took prolonged walks in Frogner Park on at least four
days a week, and quite often I would think I'd seen her,
either on the big bridge, in front of the Park Café or up
by the Monolith, but it was always someone else. I even
managed to go to the cinema in the mere hope of acci-
dentally bumping into her there. I didn't even need to
see the whole film. When the advertisements were over,
and the Orange Girl hadn't turned up, I'd sometimes just
walk out again, and then maybe buy a ticket at another
cinema. I became adept at picking out films I thought
might interest her, one of these was called 'Intersection',
and another was the Swiss film 'The Lace Maker'. But I
won't elaborate on such episodes.

There is only one connecting thread in this narrative,
Georg, and that is the times I really did meet the
enigmatic Orange Girl. There's no point highlighting all
the occasions when I didn't meet her. Just as it's pointless
to weave stories about all the Lotto tickets that haven't
won large prizes. Have you ever heard a story like that?
When did you last read a newspaper or magazine article
about the man who never became a lottery millionaire?
It's exactly the same with this story. The tale of the
Orange Girl is like the story of a huge lottery in which
only the winning tickets are visible. Just think of all the
Lotto coupons that are filled out during the course of a
week. Try picturing them all in a large room, or maybe
you'll need an entire gym hall. Then, by an elegant
sleight of hand, all the tickets that haven't won prizes of

at least ten thousand are magicked away. There won't be many tickets left in that huge hall, Georg. And they're the only ones we read about in the newspapers!

So we're on the track of the Orange Girl, it's her we're after, and she alone is everything this story is concerned with. We can forget all else for the moment. We can draw a line through all the others in the city. We can put every other woman into one huge pair of parentheses. It's that simple.

I didn't spot her before I got into the cathedral, but then I suddenly noticed her just as the organist was playing a Bach prelude. I turned to ice, I burnt with heat.

The Orange Girl was on the other side of the aisle, it couldn't be anyone but her, and also once during the service she turned and glanced up at the choir as they were singing a Christmas carol. She wasn't wearing the orange anorak this time, and there was no big bag of oranges on her lap, either. It was Christmas, after all. She was wearing a black coat and her hair was gathered at her neck by a large hair-clip of what looked like silver, yes, the purest fairytale silver; perhaps that hair-clip was fashioned by one of the seven dwarfs who, time and again, save Snow White's life.

But who was she with? There was a man sitting on her right, but not once during the service did they lean towards each other. Quite the opposite, right at the end of the service I saw the man on the right of the Orange Girl, inclining towards another woman who was sitting on his right and whispering something in her ear. I remember what a wonderful movement that was. A man can turn to his right or his left of course, it's up to him, and this man was no exception, but he turned to his right, in the right direction, you could say. I had the feeling that I was controlling which way he turned.

On the Orange Girl's left sat an plump old lady, and there was nothing to indicate that they knew each other, but of course they could have met before at the fruit market, because the old lady looked decidedly like a market trader, and perhaps they'd initiated the agreeable tradition of going to the service together. Why not, Georg? Why ever not! The Orange Girl is the market woman's best customer, or at any rate her best orange customer. And so obviously she gets her due discount. Seven kroner per kilo for Moroccan oranges, no bad price that, but the Orange Girl gets them for six-fifty – even though she spends almost half an hour filling up her bag with an assorted selection of fruits.

I didn't hear what the priest said, but presumably he spoke of Mary, Joseph and the baby Jesus, it could hardly have been otherwise. He spoke to the children; I liked that, it was their day. I was only waiting for the service to end. The postlude faded away, the congregation rose from the benches, and I had to make absolutely sure that the Orange Girl left the church before me. She passed my pew. She tossed her head slightly – I couldn't tell if she'd noticed me. But she was alone. She was even more beautiful than I remembered her. It is as if all the tinsel of Christmas had come together in one woman.

Ha! Only I knew that this young woman was a genuine Orange Girl, and therefore full of seductive secrets. I knew she had come from another fairytale with quite different rules from ours. I knew she was a spy in our world. But now she was in the cathedral as one of us, celebrating with us the birth of *our* saviour. Far from feeling it was bad, I thought it was magnanimous.

49

I followed just behind her. Outside the cathedral a few people were standing about wishing each other merry Christmas, but my gaze was fixed on the magical silver hair-clip at the Orange Girl's neck. In all the world there was only one Orange Girl, and that was because she was the only one who had found her way in here from the other reality. She was walking in the direction of Grensen now, and I followed several yards behind. It had begun to snow, frozen snowflakes dancing in the air. I only noticed because the wet flakes settled in the Orange Girl's dark hair. Her hair's getting wet, I thought, I should have an umbrella, or at least a newspaper to cover her head.

I realised it was madness, I had that much self-critical faculty left. But it was Christmas Eve. The age of miracles may be past, but we still have one magical day when anything can happen. Anything. Angels float clandestinely down, and orange girls throng the streets as if nothing untoward was happening.

Just before we reached Øvre Slottsgate I caught up with her. I walked a pace ahead, turned to her and said brightly: 'Merry Christmas!'

She obviously felt a bit taken aback, or at least she feigned it, one can never really know that sort of thing. She shot me a restrained smile. She didn't look like a spy. She looked like a girl I would have given anything to get to know better. She said: 'Merry Christmas!'

Now she was smiling properly. We began to walk on. She didn't seem to have anything against me walking along with her. I wasn't completely sure, but I thought she liked it. I could see the contours of two oranges she'd secreted under her black coat. They were identical in size and roundness. They made me nervous. They made me blush. I'd begun to get oversensitive about round shapes.

I felt I had to say something else; if I didn't I'd just have to pretend to be in a hurry and leave her. But never had time been so plentiful. I was at the very fount of time, I'd washed up at its very meaning. It put me in mind of a line from the Danish poet Piet Hein: *He, who never lives for the moment, never lives. So what of you?*

I was alive then, and it was high time, for I had never lived before. There was something inside me that was rejoicing. Before I could stop myself I had blurted out: 'So, you're not on your way to Greenland?'

It was a silly thing to say. She peered at me. 'I don't live in Greenland,' she said.

I felt terribly embarrassed, but I thought it safest to keep to the line I'd taken. 'I meant the ice-cap. With an eight-dog team and ten kilos of oranges.'

Was she smiling, or wasn't she?

It was only at that moment that it occurred to me that she might not remember me from the tram journey to Frogner. It was a disappointment, it was like losing my footing, but at the same time it was also a relief. After all, it had been a couple of months since I'd upset her bag of oranges, we'd never met before, and the whole thing had only lasted a few seconds.

But she must have remembered me from the café on Karl Johan. Or was she forever sitting in cafés holding strange men's hands? It was an unwelcome thought. It made her suspect. Even a genuine orange girl should take care not to spread her blessings about too lavishly.

'Oranges?' she repeated, smiling now with almost Mediterranean warmth, like a sirocco from the Sahara.

'Exactly,' I said, 'enough for two on a trip across Greenland.'

She had halted. I couldn't tell if she wanted our conversation to continue. I didn't know if she thought I was trying to invite her on a hazardous ski trip across Greenland. But then she looked up at me again, her dark eyes zigzagging between mine, and she asked: 'It's you, isn't it?'

I nodded, although I couldn't be absolutely certain what she'd meant, because I could hardly be the only person who'd met her with her arms full of oranges. But then she added – as if reminding herself of something: 'You were the one who bumped into me on the Frogner tram, weren't you?'

I nodded.

'You were a real twit.'

'And now that twit wants to make up for all the oranges you lost.'

She laughed lustily, as if that was the last thing she was worried about. She cocked her head to one side and said: 'Don't worry about it. You were so sweet.'

Forgive me for interrupting myself, Georg, but again I must ask you if you can help me solve a riddle. I'm sure you can see that something doesn't add up here. The Orange Girl had already sent me such a provocative look on that calamitous tram journey, an almost covetous look. She appeared to have chosen me out of all the people on that overcrowded tram, or from all the people on the face of the earth, even. Then, a few weeks later she'd let me share her café table. She'd sat for a full minute looking into my eyes before putting her hand in mine. That hand had held an entire witches' brew of delightful sensations. Then we met again just a few minutes before Christmas was rung in. But she couldn't remember me?

We shouldn't forget that she was from a different fairytale from ours, and therefore from a fairytale with very different rules. Because there were two parallel universes, the one containing our sun and the moon, the other with the unfathomable fairytale on which the Orange Girl had suddenly begun to open the door. But even so, Georg, there were only two possibilities: that she did indeed remember me vividly from both these episodes, and perhaps from the fruit market as well, but she was pretending she didn't recognise me, just feigning she'd forgotten me. That was one possibility. The other was more worrying. Listen to this: the poor girl wasn't well, she wasn't right in her mind as people say. At all events she had a serious memory impairment. Perhaps she was incapable of remembering things from one moment to the next, and possibly this is a problem common to all squirrels. A squirrel simply lives, sometimes here, sometimes there. Because 'he, who never lives for the moment, never lives. So what of you?' The playful game of life has no place for memory or reflection, it has enough to do with itself. Such was the rule in the fairytale the Orange Girl came from. By the way, I've just recalled what that fairytale was called. It was called: *come-into-my-dream*.

But on the other hand, Georg, I've since had to think about the way I might have come across to her. I, too, had sat holding her hand and looking deep into her eyes. But all I do when we meet again after a Christmas service in the cathedral is to say 'Merry Christmas', which is fair enough, but I don't make any reference to our last meeting. Far from it, I ask her if she's going to *Greenland*, with a team of eight dogs and ten kilos of oranges! What must the Orange Girl have thought of me? Perhaps she

53

concluded that I had a split personality.

We certainly talked at cross purposes. We played a complex ball game that had far too many rules. We shot and shot, but none of the balls landed in the net. Just then, Georg, an empty taxi suddenly turned in from Akersgata. The Orange Girl put out her hand, the taxi stopped, and she ran towards it . . .

I began thinking of Cinderella, who had to hurry home from the ball before the clock struck midnight, or the spell would be broken. I thought of the prince left alone on the palace balcony – deserted, alone.

But I should have known this might happen. Of course the Orange Girl had to get home before Christmas was rung in. *Those were the rules.* Orange girls didn't flit about the streets long after Christmas had been rung in. What else were bells for? Weren't they to prevent young men from being bewitched by an orange girl? The time was now a quarter to five, and soon I'd be standing alone in that godforsaken end of Øvre Slottsgate.

I was thinking fast. I only had a couple of seconds to say or do something so astute that the Orange Girl would remember me for ever.

I could ask where she lived. I could ask if we were going the same way. Or I could quickly pull out a hundred kroner for her ten kilos of oranges, including thirty for distress and inconvenience, after all, I couldn't be sure she'd got a discount. To quiet my own curiosity I could at least have asked why she continually hoarded large quantities of oranges. Not that stockpiling food was all that original. But why oranges exactly? Why not apples or bananas?

In that one second I managed to think of the ski trip across Greenland, the large family in Frogner, the end-of-

semester party with liberal helpings of orange mousse –
and the little toddler, little Ranveig, who just now lay in
the arms of a muscular father, the one who only a
fortnight ago had passed his School of Management finals
and was also a perfect Mr Know-it-all. I don't believe I
could have revisited the noisy nursery school just then.
Children had begun to make me nervous.

But I couldn't find the right words, Georg; there were
far too many to choose from. And so as she got into the
car all I blurted out was: 'I think I'm in love with you!'

It was true, but I regretted it the moment I'd said it.

The taxi drew away. But the Orange Girl wasn't inside
it. She'd changed her mind. Slowly she stepped back on
to the pavement, lifted gracefully by her own will, took
my hand – as if we'd done nothing but hold each other's
hand for the past five years – and nodded for us to start
walking again. Though she looked up at me and said: 'If
another taxi comes, I may have to take it. I'm expected
somewhere.'

By a creep of a husband and a little charm-bomb of a
baby, I thought. Or a mother and father, the father a
priest – perhaps he'd officiated at the service we'd just
come from – four sisters and two brothers, and now there
was a small puppy in the flat as well, something her kid
brother, whose name was Petter, had been nagging on
about. Or a morose and sinewy Greenland adventurer
with polar mitts, fleece suits, snowshoes, ski-wax and an
Inuit-Danish, Danish-Inuit dictionary all carefully wrapped
beneath the Christmas tree. The Orange Girl wouldn't be
going to any end-of-semester celebration tonight. Tonight
she had time off from the nursery school.

'They'll soon be ringing Christmas in, won't they?' I
said. 'You mustn't be in the city after Christmas has been

rung in.'

She made no reply to that, she just squeezed my hand firmly and tenderly – as if we were soaring weightlessly about in space, as if we'd drunk our fill of intergalactic milk and had the entire universe to ourselves.

We had passed the History Museum and had arrived at the Palace park. I knew that another taxi might appear at any moment. I knew that the church bells would soon be ringing in the Christmas festivities.

I stopped and stood before her. Gently, I stroked her damp hair and let my hand rest on the silver hair-clip at her neck. It was ice cold, but it warmed my body all the same. Imagine! I was the one who was touching it!

Then I said: 'When can we see each other again?'

She stood looking down at the pavement before raising her eyes to me. Her pupils were dancing uneasily, and I thought her lips were trembling. Then she set me a riddle I was to ponder a lot in the time to come. She said: 'How long can you wait?'

How was I to answer that question, Georg? Perhaps it was a trap. If I answered 'two or three days', I might seem over-eager. And if I answered 'my whole life', she might think that either I wasn't genuinely fond of her, or simply that I wasn't genuine. So I had to find something in between.

'I can wait until my heart bleeds with sorrow,' I said.

She sent me a flickering smile. She ran her finger across my lips. Then she said: 'And how long is that?'

I shook my head dejectedly and decided to say just what I felt. 'Perhaps only another five minutes.'

She was clearly pleased with my answer, but she countered in a whisper: 'It would be good if you could wait a little longer . . .'

Now it was my turn to demand an answer. 'How long?'

'You must be able to wait six months,' she said. 'If you can manage to wait that long, we can see each other again.'

I think I sighed. 'Why *so* long?'

The Orange Girl's face tensed. It was as if she had to force herself to be hard. 'Because that's just how long you've *got* to wait.'

She saw how the disappointment hit me. Perhaps that was why she added: 'But if you manage that, we can be together every day for the whole of the next six months.'

The church bells began to ring, and only then did I remove my hand from the wet hair and the silver hair-clip. At that moment an empty taxi drove up Wergelandsveien. It had to be.

She looked me in the eyes, seemed to beg me for something, for understanding, to use all my faculties and wits. Again her eyes had tears in them. 'Well, happy Christmas . . . Jan Olav!' she stammered. Then she hailed the taxi, got in and waved elatedly to me. But destiny hung heavily in the atmosphere. She didn't turn to look round as the taxi sped away and disappeared. I thought she was crying.

I was overcome, Georg. I was in shock. I'd won a million on the Lotto, but only for a few minutes, till they discovered something wrong with the ticket and the prize money couldn't be paid out, at least not right away.

Who was this transcendental Orange Girl? It was a question I'd asked myself many times before. But now a new question had presented itself. *How did she know what my name was?*

The bells of the cathedral and all the other churches in the city centre were still ringing; they were ringing for the Christmas festivities. There was no one else about in the streets, and perhaps because of that I shouted out the same question again and again into the December air, in a high voice, almost as if I were singing: 'How did she know my name?' Just as pressing was another question: why did six months have to elapse before she would see me again?

I was to have ample time to consider that question. And gradually, as the days wore on, I was never at a loss for possible answers, I just couldn't tell which might turn out to be the right one. I had precious few symptoms to go on, but even then, as you know, I was good at reading signs and making diagnoses. Perhaps I was a bit too enthusiastic. There were too many parallel theories.

Possibly the Orange Girl really was seriously ill, and perhaps someone had put her on a strict orange diet for that reason. Perhaps she was to undergo some painful medical treatment in America or Switzerland for the next six months, as no one here at home could do anything more for her. Her eyes were always filling with tears, especially whenever she tore herself away from me. But she had also hinted that we could see one another every day for the rest of the new year, in other words from July to December. I was first to wait six months for the Orange Girl, and then I was to be with her *every day* after that. The thought of it inspired me. It was a pretty good deal, and really I had no reason to moan. It actually meant that we would see one another every other day during the coming year. Wouldn't it have been infinitely worse if we'd *first* been able to see each other every day for six months and then never met again?

58

I'd just begun studying medicine, and it's a well-known fact that medical students often tend to 'see' imaginary diseases in themselves and others, so eager are they to read symptoms in an almost detective-like desire to make diagnoses. Just as it isn't unusual for theology students to begin to doubt their belief in God, or for law students to start talking a critical view of their country's laws and jurisprudence. So as a matter of rigid self-discipline, I tried to lay aside the idea that the Orange Girl was seriously ill and was going for some unpleasant treatment abroad. There were more than enough other theories to follow up.

For example, even if the Orange Girl had been really ill, or not in her right mind, how would that have explained the way she knew my name? And why did she start crying practically every time she saw me? What was it about me that made her so inexpressibly melancholy?

At this point, and unselfconsciously, I might have begun to initiate you in all the fictions I spun during the days of that Christmas holiday. I might, for example, pass on everything I invented about that large family in Frogner. Or I might begin listing all the reasons I uncovered that prevented me meeting the Orange Girl again for another six months. One of these answers, and pretty typical of its kind, was that the Orange Girl was just too good for this world. She travelled to Africa in secret to smuggle food and medicine to the poorest people of that huge continent, particularly in the regions where malaria and other awful diseases wreaked havoc. Such an answer still didn't solve the riddle of all the oranges. But why not, though? Perhaps she was going to take them with her to Africa. Why hadn't I thought of that? Maybe all her

59

savings had gone towards chartering a Hercules plane.

But, Georg, we have already agreed that we only need to follow the real clues about the Orange Girl. If I revealed all the thoughts and fancies I gradually wove around her, I'd have to sit at my computer for a whole year, and I haven't got that long. It's as simple as that, although it pains me to think of it.

But why concentrate on fantasies? Apart from the rare occasions the Orange Girl had looked into my eyes, the couple of times she'd held my hand, and the single moment she'd stroked my lips with her finger, really the only things I had to hold on to were the few words we'd exchanged. So it was important to get clear exactly what had been said. I was quick to write out our exchanges, and I tried to rack my brains to interpret them.

How are you doing, Georg? Can you: 1) Say why she bought so many oranges; 2) tell me why she looked deep into my eyes and held my hand in the café without saying so much as a word; 3) say why she studied each and every orange she brought at Youngstorget fruit market – perhaps to prevent any two looking identical; 4) discover any clues as to why we couldn't see each other for six months; and 5) guess the biggest conundrum of all, how she knew my name.

If you manage to solve this rebus, you will presumably be well on the way to answering the cardinal question: who *was* the Orange Girl? Was she one of us? Or was she from a completely different reality, from another world perhaps, a world she had to return to for half a year before she could come back and settle amongst us.

I couldn't read the clues, Georg. I couldn't make any diagnosis.

Not long after the Orange Girl had driven away up Wergelandsveien, another taxi came along, and I took it. I went home to Humleveien to celebrate Christmas with my family.

Einar's one passion that winter was slalom skiing. I'd bought him some rugged skiing mitts and looked forward to seeing him unwrap them after Christmas dinner. I'd also bought a tin of gourmet food for his cat. My mother was to get a much discussed Finnish anthology. It was written by Märta Tikkanen and was called *Love Story of the Century*. Dad was to get a novel called *Dead Run* by the Norwegian first-time author Erling Gjelsvik. I had recently read the book myself and reckoned it might be something for Dad. But there was more to it than that. In those days I nursed the dream of writing something myself one day. Perhaps that was why I got an extra little kick from giving my father a book by a young writer who was making his debut.

At the time I was the one who used to sleep in the little room off the living room. Now it's your room, at least at the time of writing it is. As regards the time of reading, I'm completely in the dark.

I'm going to keep to the rules we've laid down for this narrative and not say anything about that year's Christmas celebrations. All I'm going to divulge is that I couldn't sleep a wink the night of Christmas Eve.

I'd only got halfway through Dad's letter, but I had to visit the loo. It was my own fault. It was because I'd had all that Coke, of course.

Damn! I thought. Now I'd have to go through the living room, lobby and hall with inquisitive glances from all sides.

I think it's known as 'running the gauntlet'. But I had no choice.

I unlocked my door, left the printout lying on the bed, and locked the door after me. I put the key in my pocket.

All four of them were on my case immediately. I tried to pretend I wasn't worried about all the curious looks that came my way.

'Have you finished already?' Mum asked. She looked like one large living question mark. What was it I'd been reading?

'Was it a bit sad?' hazarded Jørgen. He wanted to show he felt sorry for me because my dad had died, although he'd always done his best to be a good replacement. Well, I suppose that's all right, but he could hardly feel sorry for Mum, who'd lost her husband, and at the time take her husband's place, not to mention his bed. I think, deep down, that Jørgen was pleased Dad died. If he hadn't he would never have had Mum. If he hadn't, he would never have had Miriam. And if he hadn't, he would never have had me for that matter. There is a saying that goes: 'one man's meat is another man's poison'.

I saw that he'd poured himself a large glass of whisky. He does have a glass sometimes, but only on Fridays and Saturdays. This was a Monday.

I don't think he felt particularly embarrassed about standing around the living room with a stiff drink, at least that isn't why I mentioned the fact. But perhaps he was a bit diffident because I'd locked myself in my room to read something my real Dad had written to me just before he died, and long before Jørgen came on the scene. When I was younger there were times when I called Jørgen a 'newcomer'. That was childish, I only did it to annoy him.

'Or is there more to read?' Grandpa asked. He'd lit a cigar. He'd got hold of the right end of the stick.

'I've only read half of it,' I said. 'I'm just going to the loo.'

'But are you *enjoying* what you're reading?' Grandma probed.

'No comment!' I said. That's what politicians say to journalists when they don't want to answer difficult questions.

The similarity between journalists and parents is that they're equally nosy. And the similarity between politicians and children is that they're forever being bombarded with delicate questions that aren't always easy to answer.

Perhaps it's about time I introduced the characters in this story a little better, and I'll begin with my mother as she's the one I know best, after all.

Mum won't see forty again, and I can describe her as a mature and independent woman; at least, she's never afraid to speak her mind. She's also 'maternal' and I'm not just thinking about the way she looks after Miriam. She coddles me rather a lot too, and sometimes she talks to me as if I were two or three years younger than I am. I don't usually bother about it, but sometimes it does affect me, for example when I bring friends home from school. It's as if she enjoys showing them that I'm her darling little boy, even though I'm an inch or two taller than her. Once when I was in the living room playing chess with a friend called Martin, she came over to the sofa and started brushing my hair! I said what I thought pretty forcefully. I don't like being cross with Mum – and that time I was more than cross, I was ballistic – but I had to take account of Martin being there; I had to show him that I was capable of imposing limits. Mum retreated into the kitchen, but twenty minutes later she was back with hot chocolate and Christmas cake. Martin gave a whistle of approval, but after what had already happened I found it embarrassing that she should look after us like that. For two pins I'd have run into the kitchen to see if I could find a beer in the fridge. And if there wasn't any beer, I at least knew where Jørgen kept his whisky bottle. Luckily, Martin has a sense of humour, and of course we talked about what had happened afterwards. I think his respect for Mum grew a bit when I told him that she taught at the National Academy of Fine Arts. 'If another Picasso suddenly emerges, you'll know where he got it from,' I said. After what had happened it was in my own interests to build her up a bit.

It's hard to describe your mother, at least as regards virtues and vices and suchlike, but there are certain things that do specially stand out. Mum loves liquorice, and I mean all kinds of liquorice. I come across liquorice boats, cartons of Frazer liquorice and Liquorice Allsorts everywhere. Recently she's started to become a closet liquorice eater because both Jørgen and I have got to grips with the problem and confronted her with her bad habit. Jørgen thinks you can get high blood pressure from eating liquorice, and although that may be a bit of an exaggeration, things have got to the point where she's made me promise not to say anything to Jørgen when we've been in town and she's bought herself a bag of liquorice boats or a fix of Allsorts.

If I was asked to describe Mum's best characteristic in two words it would be 'good temper'. But then, I'd also have to admit that her worst point is 'bad temper'. I don't often experience many intermediate shades between these two extremes. Mum is usually in bright good humour, but occasionally she can be really miserable. So she's always in some humour, but it's never 'middling'. Mum's favourite line is 'Let's have a game of cards before we go to bed.'

Then there's Jørgen. He's only five foot seven, the same height as Mum, so he's not all that big for an adult man. Many people would view this as a handicap, and if so, it's not his only one, because Jørgen has red hair, too. He has pale skin, never goes brown in the summer, just bright red and sunburnt, and has this red hair; even the hairs on his arms are red. I've already mentioned that he's fashion conscious, even to the point of being a bit affected. Most men don't have three deodorants and four brands of aftershave lotion on their bathroom shelves. Nor would many of them dare to go into town dressed in a black silk scarf and a bright yellow camel-hair jacket. But Jørgen does. The worst thing is, it suits him.

Despite all this, Jørgen works as a police investigator at KRIPOS – the National Bureau of Crime Investigation! He's constantly telling us he's got a 'duty of confidentiality', but he can't always manage to keep quiet. On at least two occasions I've learnt vital details of important criminal investigations before they've been reported in the press. It shows he trusts me. That's a fine trait. Jørgen knows I won't go rushing around letting out police secrets.

Jørgen is the type who thinks he knows best, but he isn't always right. Some time ago we went to IKEA and bought a new wardrobe for my room. (There had been a number of complaints about my clothes lying about all over the house; a slight exaggeration because I haven't so much as jettisoned a sock upstairs. The truth is I hardly ever set foot up there.) Putting the IKEA wardrobe together took all afternoon, and then we spent the whole evening positioning it. Jørgen's idea was that the wardrobe should stand against the wall behind the door, but I totally disagreed. I thought it should go next to the window even though it cut out a quarter of an inch of the view. I said it was my room and I wasn't worried about losing a quarter of an inch of the view. I reminded him that I'd lived here a lot longer than he had, and I didn't think it was practical to have a wardrobe you couldn't get at when the bedroom door was open. Of course, I got my own way, but it was almost a whole day before he spoke to me again, and when at last he did, it was obvious he was having to make an effort.

Perhaps Jørgen's best quality is that he's willing to spend almost all his spare time making me athletic. Everyone is born with muscles, he says, but muscles are there to be used. His worst quality must be his refusal to accept that I have plans to be something other than a sportsman. I don't think Jørgen sets much store by my constant practising of the Moonlight Sonata. Without doubt Jørgen's favourite line is: 'It's the attitude that counts!'

Before I say anything about Grandma and Grandpa, I should emphasise that I know them very well, every bit as well as I know Jørgen, because over the years I've stayed with them in Tønsberg quite a lot. This was particularly the case when Mum and Jørgen were going out together. I was only ten then. I don't think Mum and Jørgen would have become proper lovers at all if they hadn't been able to farm me out for a few days or weeks at a time. I'm not trying to complain or anything, quite the opposite. I've always enjoyed going to Tønsberg. I'm also glad that Mum and Jørgen had the sense to shield me from the early, introductory phase of their relationship, i.e. the flirting. There was enough to adjust to without that. Once, when I went upstairs to say goodnight, I saw them lying under the duvet necking. I didn't like seeing that, so I just turned round and crept downstairs. Maybe I'd have reacted differently if Jørgen had been my real dad. And maybe not. I didn't actually find it all that disgusting, but they could have closed the bedroom door. They could have said they were going to bed. Then I wouldn't have felt so silly. I wouldn't have felt so lonely.

Grandma – my dad's mother – will soon be seventy and has been a singing teacher most of her life. She loves music of every sort, but most of all Puccini. Grandma sees it as her life's work to get me to like *La Bohème*, but to be honest I find Italian opera too gooey, and *La Bohème* is no exception; it's just one great jumble of romance and tuberculosis. Apart from that, Grandma is a great nature lover, and she's particularly interested in birds. She's well keen on all kinds of seafood and has invented a special shellfish salad, which she's christened 'Tønsberg salad'. (Prawns, crab meat and fish balls. The original bit is the fish balls.) Every autumn she wants me to go out picking mushrooms with her. Most positive characteristic: Grandma knows the names of all the birds and where they build their nests. Worst characteristic: unfortunately she's incapable of making food without singing an aria from Puccini. I've never tried to wean her off it, to be honest I haven't dared, because Grandma makes fantastic food. Favourite line: 'Sit down here, Georg, and we'll have a little chat.'

Before Grandpa retired he was a meteorologist, and he still hasn't given this interest up, as he buys *Verdens Gang* every day just to discuss the weather forecast of a particularly nice-looking female meteorologist. He smokes cigars, but only at parties according to him. He obviously defines every visit I make to Tønsberg as a party, likewise each time we go out in the boat. He is a very jolly, jokey man, effer-vescent even, and he's never afraid to speak his mind. If he thinks Grandma's hair looks awful, he isn't afraid to say so. But he won't hesitate to say her hair looks nice either. Grandpa spends half the summer on his 'island-hopper' motor boat and the winter on the newspapers. Sometimes he writes an article for the local paper, the *Tønsberg Blad*, and he could be said to be one of Tønsberg's celebrities. Best side: Grandpa is fantastic fun at sea. Weakest side: he sometimes seems to think he's the king of Tønsberg. Favourite line: 'We rich are doing all right!'

Uncle Einar has been mentioned a couple of times, too. I think it was rather fun to read that he was the same age as me the autumn my dad met the Orange Girl. Now he's the first officer of a large merchant ship and a bachelor, but rumour has it that he has a girlfriend in every port. (For a while I had a suspicion that he had a girlfriend aboard as well. At least there was an 'Ingrid' who sailed with him for six months, before she suddenly went ashore.) Several times he's promised to let me do some travelling on his ship, but I'm sure it's all talk because nothing has ever come of it. Strongest point: he's presumably Norway's coolest uncle. Weakest: never keeps his promises. Favourite rejoinder: 'You haven't been to sea yet, lad!'

There is only one person left, and he's the most difficult of all to describe, because it's Georg Røed. I'm five foot nine, a couple of inches taller than Jørgen. I don't think he likes that much, but perhaps he'll rise above it (!). As I'm inside this person I can't watch him moving around the room. Sometimes, though, I do meet him face to face, on the odd occasions when I'm standing in front of a mirror. It may sound funny, but I really do belong to that group of people who are reasonably happy about their appearance. I wouldn't say that I'm good looking, but at least I'm not particularly ugly. I have to be a bit careful here. I read somewhere that over twenty per cent of all women think they're among the three per cent of most beautiful women in the country, and those figures don't add up. I wouldn't know how many people think they're amongst the three per cent of the ugliest individuals, but it must be terrible to be unhappy about the person you are, all through your life. I sincerely hope that Jørgen doesn't go round feeling unhappy because he has red hair and is only five foot seven in his socks. It's something I've wondered about occasionally, but I've never dared to ask him directly.

The closest I get to an anxiety about my appearance is that I've begun to get some embarrassing pimples on my forehead, and the idea that they may disappear in four or eight years time isn't much comfort. Jørgen maintains that they may disappear after a few good jogs with him, but I don't buy that. Anyway, it was rather a silly thing for him to say, as now I certainly won't start pounding the tarmac. Jørgen would only think I'd begun to jog because I wanted to be rid of my pimples.

I've inherited blue eyes from my father, got fair hair and fairly light skin, but I turn a good brown colour in summer. Best attribute: Georg Røed belongs to that section of the global community that actually realises we're living on a planet in the Milky Way. Worst attribute: not exactly brilliant with girls. I wouldn't mind getting a bit more positive on that front. Favourite words: 'Yes, please, a bit more of both.'

After going to the loo I had to brave the living room again, but this time none of the others said anything. They'd obviously agreed they wouldn't. I opened the door to the room that had once been my father's, locked it behind me and threw myself down on the bed. Soon now I'd discover who the mysterious Orange Girl was. If my dad ever saw her again, that was. Maybe she was a witch. She'd certainly managed to bewitch Dad. There had to be a reason why it was so important for him to tell me about her. Obviously there was something I had to know, something very important for my dad to tell his son before he died.

I hadn't quite got rid of the feeling that this Orange Girl had something to do with the Hubble Space Telescope in one way or another, or at least with the universe and space. Dad had written something odd, something that had rekindled this notion. I flipped back and read it again: . . . *she just squeezed my hand firmly and tenderly – as if we were soaring weightlessly about in space, as if we'd drunk our fill of intergalactic milk and had the entire universe to ourselves.*

Could the Orange Girl have come from another planet? There was at least the hint that she came from a world other than ours. Perhaps she came from a UFO? No, of course she didn't, I didn't believe in them, and Dad certainly didn't either. But perhaps she thought she had! That would be almost as bad.

The Hubble Space Telescope takes ninety-seven minutes to orbit the earth at a speed of 28,000 kilometres an hour. By comparison, the first steam train between Oslo and Eidsvoll took two and a half hours for the sixty-eight-kilometre journey. I've worked out that its average speed was about twenty-eight kilometres an hour. So therefore the Hubble Space Telescope is a thousand times faster than Norway's first train. (My teacher thought this was a very inventive comparison!)

28,000 kilometres an hour! That really is floating weight-lessly about in space! Perhaps you might also talk about drinking your fill of 'intergalactic milk', at least whenever pictures are taken of galaxies millions of light years away from the Milky Way.

The Hubble Space Telescope has two wings made up of solar panels. They're twelve metres long and two and a half metres wide and supply the satellite with 3,000 watts of power. But those two turtle doves coming from the cathedral could hardly have perched, one on each wing of the Hubble Space Telescope, and had all of the universe to themselves before they passed by the History Museum and got up to the Palace park. But who knows, they may have been in Seventh Heaven.

I picked up the sheaf of papers and read on.

I made no attempt to search for the Orange Girl between Christmas and the New Year. Some deference had to be paid to the tranquillity of Christmas. But it wasn't far into January when I took up the chase. I was on top form.

I made hundreds of attempts to trace her, but none of them succeeded, and so I've nothing to tell. I'm certain that by now you're quite used to the rhythm and logic of this story.

But I'm going to make one exception, though, and this is in connection with an important item I forgot to mention in my little list of riddles for you to solve. That old anorak, Georg! What about that? It had been largely responsible for suggesting the strenuous trip across Greenland to my imagination. From an early stage it had made me assume that the Orange Girl might be very poor. But first and foremost, of course, it was a sign that she was an outdoor type.

I went on lots of skiing hikes that winter, and perhaps it's partly due to all that exercise in the forests and mountains around Oslo that my body has been able to keep the virulent disease at bay for some months. It isn't the skiing trips I want to speak about here, because I never saw her out there, not on the pistes nor at the huts. But by the beginning of March, Holmenkollen Sunday was approaching. The thought of the approaching ski-jumping championship filled me with anticipation. It was as if all the pieces had come together, the whole jigsaw. It was like having eleven right on the football pools, with only one game to go, and that was a dead certainty.

When the weather is fine, more than 50,000 people turn up for the Sunday events at Holmenkollen. A considerable portion of Oslo's population climbs the hill that day. But Oslo's population of old anorak wearers – what sort of percentage do you think there is of them? Not far short of one hundred per cent, if you ask me.

I went to Holmenkollen that Sunday and the weather wasn't too bad, it was almost a dead 'cert'. I had more than 50,000 chances of meeting the Orange Girl, and I can tell you one thing: there was no shortage of old anoraks on the roof of Oslo that March Sunday; every one of them was there. A Sunday at Holmenkollen is like an El Dorado of ancient anoraks of every sunbleached hue. I didn't even glance at the jumping – I had more than enough to do looking at all the anoraks. I found the Orange Girl a number of times, and each time a real Holmenkollen roar was building in my breast, but it was never her. A couple of times I even caught sight of that enchanting hair-clip as well, but not on her head.

She wasn't there, Georg. That was the truth. And that was all I got out of it. I didn't even register who'd won. I noticed nothing that Sunday except that the Orange Girl was missing. I only had eyes for what wasn't there.

Since then, I've only been to Holmenkollen once, and I don't know if that rings any bells with you. Is it possible you have a vague recollection of something we did together when you were just three and a half?

This year you and I stood down on the level and looked up at all the ski-jumpers. The weather on that March day was quite unique. A rare, mild wind had sighed over the country bringing temperatures that were almost summery. The snow for the huge ski-jump had to be transported halfway across the country, or from the mountains near Finse to be more exact. This year it was Jens Weissflog who won the gold. It was a real blow for the Norwegian spectators, but it didn't cause much of a sensation, because Weissflog had run off with the gold last year as well.

I'll let you into a little secret. Even on that mild March day nearly six months ago when we were at Holmenkollen, I caught myself time and time again looking round for the Orange Girl. More than a decade had passed, but that disappoinment still lived on within me.

I haven't got much time, young Georg. But that's not the only reason I'm going to jump a few weeks ahead. There isn't any more to tell before we get there.

Suddenly, one day at the end of April, I found myself picking up a lovely postcard from our postbox. It was a Saturday and I was visiting my parents in Humleveien. The card hadn't been sent to Adamstuen where I'd been sharing accommodation with Gunnar for some months, and yet it was for me.

Just listen to this: on the front of the card was a picture of a wonderful orange grove with PATIO DE LOS NARANJOS printed in large letters. It means

73

something like *the orange courtyard*, that much Spanish I could understand. I was good at putting things together as I've said.

The orange courtyard! My heart began pounding in my chest. There's a thing called blood pressure, Georg. In extreme situations it can suddenly shoot right up, sometimes in one bound. But don't let that keep you away from great experiences and deep impressions. It's a harmless reaction. (Even so, I'd prefer you not to take up hang-gliding or parachuting. And avoid bungee-jumping at all costs!)

I turned the card over. It was postmarked Seville, and the only thing written on it was: *I've been thinking of you. Can you wait a little longer?*

There was nothing more and there was no name or sender's address either. But a face had been painted on the card. It was her face, Georg, the squirrel face. It looked as if it had been painted by an artist, and a good one at that.

I wasn't really all that taken aback. Naturally the Orange Girl was in the Orange Courtyard; where else should she be? She had simply gone back to her own queenly realm, to Orange Land. It fitted all too well with my preconceptions. Hadn't Jesus, too, stayed in the temple to be in his father's house?

Nothing was incomprehensible any more. All riddles were solved. The solitaire had come out. Down there the Orange Girl could draw breath for six months and cultivate her discriminating, almost artistic passion for the multifariousness of the orange, before hopefully being sufficiently revived to tear herself away and keep her promise to see me every day for the next six months. Then perhaps she'd have to go down and charge herself

74

up again, but that was something for later on.

I was elated, and my brain began to produce too much of a chemical we doctors call endorphins. There is a special word for this almost clinical state of elation. We say that the patient is *euphoric*. This was the state I found myself in now. The result was that I rushed in to Mum and Dad. They were both sitting in the conservatory, Mum in the green rocking-chair and Dad ensconced behind the Saturday paper on the old chaise longue. I tumbled in and announced that I was going to be married. That's what I said, I explained that I intended to get married. I shouldn't have done it, because only a quarter of an hour later the reaction set in. My brain stopped producing endorphins all together, and I wasn't euphoric any longer. I understood nothing. I understood less than I'd ever done.

The Orange Girl had already revealed that she knew my first name. But now it appeared that she knew my surname as well. And more than that, Georg. Down in Orange Land she'd also had a note of the address of the old house in Humleveien. What about that? It was beautiful, it was lovely to think about, regardless of the explanation of the riddle itself. But wasn't there a bitter twist, too, in that she'd gone all the way to Spain without even bothering to mention it to me in those magic moments when we'd been walking hand in hand towards the Palace park before Christmas rang in and Cinderella had to leap into her carriage only seconds before it was turned into a pumpkin?

That was three and a half months and at least twenty-five skiing trips, or should I say search parties, ago.

Or had the Orange Girl been in Morocco, California and Brazil as well? Today the orange is a global commodity, Georg, and as far as I'm concerned it should have been elevated to the position of nature's most important fruit a long time ago. Perhaps the Orange Girl worked undercover for the UN's Inspectorate of Oranges (UNIO). Could a wholly new and horrendous orange disease have developed? Was that why she was constantly at the Youngstorget fruit market inspecting the condition of the oranges? Was that why she took her weekly random samples?

Perhaps she'd been all the way to China. I'd found out long before that the orange originally came from China. But if the Orange Girl had gone on a pilgrimmage all the way to China, where once the planet's first orange flower had blossomed, I still could never have sent a postcard with an address like *The Orange Girl, China*. It would have been much too difficult for the Chinese postman to find her amongst more than a billion other people. I should have succeeded all right, but I couldn't guarantee that the Chinese postman would be as diligent as me.

Well, Georg, we must press on.

I tore myself away from my studies for a few days, borrowed a thousand kroner from Mum and Dad and got hold of a cheap air ticket to Madrid. There I stayed overnight with the uncle of an old classmate. Early next morning I flew on to Seville.

Of course I couldn't be sure of finding her, though I reckoned that the odds were about as good as finding her at Holmenkollen. But there was something else, too: even if I didn't meet her face to face in Seville, I was at least secure in the knowledge that she'd been there fairly recently – before she went on to Morocco, for example. At all events I'd be able to experience Orange Land, and breathe in some of the same tangy orange scent that she had inhaled. I wanted to walk in the same streets she'd walked in, perhaps I'd sit on the same benches she'd sat on. That, on its own, was more than enough reason to travel. And it wasn't inconceivable that I might come across some important clues she'd left behind, perhaps in the Orange Courtyard itself, if I was able to get in. I imagined there might be moats, ferocious dogs and strict patrols around such a holy site.

But barely half an hour after I'd landed in Seville I was able to stroll right into the Orange Courtyard. It lay nestling in the lee of the huge cathedral and was a lovely, enclosed orange grove, almost like a formal garden. Orange trees stood lined up in rows replete with overripe fruit.

But the Orange Girl wasn't there. Presumably she'd just slipped out to the town. She'd soon be back . . .

I tried to think straight. I tried to tell myself that I couldn't expect to meet the Orange Girl straight away, perhaps not even during my first few days. So I didn't stay in the Orange Courtyard for more than three hours. But before I went, I left a note for her on an old fountain in the middle of the orchard for safety's sake. *I've been thinking of you as well*, I wrote. *No, I can't wait any longer.* I placed a pebble on top of the note.

I didn't sign my name, I didn't even write on it who the note was for, but I added a little matchstick drawing of my face. It was no likeness at all, but I felt sure the Orange Girl would understand what the drawing was meant to represent when she found the note. It couldn't be long before she was back. She must at least pop in now and again to collect her post.

★

It was scarcely an hour later, when I was well into the city again, that I realised with a pang of dismay that I might have done something terribly wrong.

She'd said: *You must be able to wait six months. If you can manage to wait that long, we can see each other again.* Then I'd asked why I had to wait so long, and the Orange Girl had simply replied: *Because that's just how long you've got to wait. But if you manage that, we can be together every day for the whole of the next six months.*

Do you see, Georg? I hadn't followed the rules. I hadn't managed to wait six months for her. And so I no longer had her word that we could be together every day for the next six months.

The solemn pact we'd entered into had been simple enough to understand, it was just so hard to keep. But all fairytales have rules, and perhaps it's their rules that actually distinguish one fairytale from another. These rules never need to be *understood*. They only need to be followed. If not, what they promise won't come true!

Do you see, Georg? Why did Cinderella have to be back from the ball before midnight? I haven't a clue, and I'm sure Cinderella didn't either. But one isn't allowed to ask about such things once one has been transported into the most wondrous dream world by the touch of a wand. One must simply accept the conditions, however incomprehensible they seem. If Cinderella is to get the prince, she must tear herself away from the ball before midnight. It's as simple and straightforward as that. She must abide by the rules. If not, she'll lose her ball gown, and her carriage will get turned into a pumpkin. And so she ensures she gets home before the stroke of twelve – she just makes it – losing only a glass slipper on the way.

Oddly enough, it's this slipper that leads the prince to her in the end. The two ugly sisters *did* break the rules, and they really got it in the neck.

Other rules applied in this fairytale. If I just managed to spot the Orange Girl with a large bag of oranges in her arms three times in a row, she'd be mine. But I also had to catch a glimpse of her on Christmas Eve and, furthermore, I had to make sure I was looking into her eyes and touching her magical silver hair-clip at the moment Christmas was rung in. After that, there was only one test left: I must be able to endure not seeing her for six months. Don't ask why, Georg, but those were the rules. If I didn't manage the final, decisive one – keeping away from the the Orange Girl for half a year – all my previous efforts would be in vain, and all would be lost.

I rushed back to the Orange Orchard. But the note had gone, and I couldn't even be certain that she'd taken it. It could just as easily have been picked up by a Norwegian tourist.

Just as my eye lighted on the pebble I'd laid over the now missing note, a new thought struck me. It was something that gave me a glimmer of hope, even though I hadn't obeyed the rules. Well, Georg, the Orange Girl had written to me first because she had my address. Then I'd written a note to her in reply, but as I had no address to send it to, I had to bring it courier-fashion to the same Orange Courtyard she'd sent her greeting from.

Weren't we in a sense equally culpable? Hadn't she broken some rules as well? What do you think, Georg? You can interpret the rules of this fairytale as well as I can.

But on the other hand, she had begged me to *wait a little longer*. She'd really done no more than renew our pact. And I had replied that I *couldn't* accept the conditions, and was therefore no longer going to keep to the rules.

She had written: *I've been thinking of you. Can you wait a little longer?*

But, Georg, if the answer to that question was that I couldn't, what did she expect me to do then?

I was in no position to make a judgement about it. I was far too personally involved. All I could do was try to find her.

I'd never been to Seville before; I'd never even been to Spain. But soon I was following the stream of tourists up to the old Jewish quarter of the city. It was called *Santa Cruz* and looked almost like a huge temple dedicated to the orange as a traditional plant. At any rate, all the plazas and market places were lined with orange trees.

After moving from plaza to plaza without finding the Orange Girl, I finally sat down at a café, where I found an empty chair in the shade of a luxuriant orange tree. I had been to all the plazas in Santa Cruz and made up my mind that this was the loveliest of them all. It was called Plaza de la Alianza.

I sat there mulling over a problem: if you're looking for a person in a large city and have no idea of their whereabouts, is it best to move around from place to place, or is the chance of meeting them greater if you sit down in a central location and wait until they turn up of their own accord?

Read that sentence twice before giving your opinion, Georg. But I came to the conclusion that the best part of Seville was Santa Cruz, and that the finest of its squares was the Plaza de la Alianza. If the Orange Girl was anything like me, sooner or later she'd have to turn up just where I was sitting. We'd met each other at a café in Oslo. And we'd met each other at the cathedral. If there was one thing the Orange Girl and I were good at, it was bumping into one another fortuitously.

I decided to sit where I was. It was only three o'clock so I could sit in the Plaza de la Alianza for at least eight hours more. I didn't consider that was long to wait. Before I left Oslo I'd booked a room at a small guest house close by. They'd told me that I'd have to be in before midnight, because that was when they locked the doors. (Even Spanish guest houses have rules that have to be followed!) If the Orange Girl didn't show up by ten to twelve that first evening, I made up my mind I'd sit in the same square all the following day, too. I could sit there from sunrise to sunset.

I waited and waited. I looked at all the people who came and went in the square, locals and tourists alike. I was struck by what a beautiful place the world was. Again I got a feeling of euphoria linked to everything around me. Who are we who live here? Every single person in the plaza was like a living treasure full of thoughts and memories, dreams and desires. I was engrossed in my own little life on earth, but that applied to everyone else in the plaza as well. The waiter, for instance, was engrossed in serving all his customers, and after I'd ordered my fourth cup of coffee, I got the feeling that he thought I'd occupied the table for long enough; it had been over three hours since I'd sat down. After another half hour, when the fourth cup was empty, he was quickly on the spot asking politely if I'd care to pay. But I couldn't go, I was waiting for the Orange Girl and so, for safety's sake, I ordered a large portion of tapas and a Coke. No beer or wine before the Orange Girl came, I decided – we were going to drink champagne. But no Orange Girl appeared. The clock turned seven, and now I felt forced to ask for the bill. Suddenly I realised how naive I'd been. It had been many days since I'd found that postcard in the mailbox at Hunleveien, and it had taken as least as long again to get there.

The Orange Girl seemed just as unattainable as before. Clearly she had better things to do than play cat and mouse with me; perhaps she was studying Spanish at Salamanca or Madrid. I'd paid my dues at the café, I was ready to go. I was disappointed in my own defective sense of judgement and, with a lump in my throat, I made up my mind to travel home to Norway the very next morning.

I don't know if you've ever had that intense feeling of having done something completely futile. Maybe you've left home in awful weather and gone into town to buy something you really need, and you get to the shop at last only to find it had closed two minutes ago. Such things are infuriating, and most irritating of all is one's own stupidity. It was this almost embarrassing feeling of having journeyed in vain that had gripped me now, and I hadn't just caught a bus into town. I'd come all the way to Seville with only a picture postcard to go by, I didn't know anyone here, I was just about to book into a dirty little guest house, and I couldn't speak a word of Spanish. I felt like giving myself a real clip on the ear, but that would have looked so silly that I'd only have felt more ashamed, so I swore to punish myself in some other way. There were many forms that punishment could take. For instance, I could swear to myself that no matter what happened in later life, I'd have nothing whatever to do with the Orange Girl.

82

And then she came, Georg. It was seven thirty, and suddenly she turned up in the Plaza de la Alianza!

Four and a half hours after I'd sat down under the orange tree, the Orange Girl came fluttering in to the orange plaza. Not in her old anorak, of course – Andalucia is sub-tropical. She was dressed in a little fairytale of a summer frock, which glowed as red as the bougainvillaea that festooned a high wall in the background and had long attracted my admiration. Perhaps she'd borrowed Sleeping Beauty's dress, I thought, or pinched it from one of the fairies.

She hadn't seen me. Darkness had begun to fall over the plaza. It was hot, very hot, but even so I felt cold, I shuddered.

But then, Georg – I mustn't keep anything from you – I realised she'd come into the square with a young man of perhaps twenty-five. He looked tall and good-looking and sported a full, fair beard. He looked exactly like some polar traveller. What worried me most, though, was that he didn't seem at all unsympathetic.

So, I had lost. But it was my own fault. I hadn't followed the rules. I had broken a solemn undertaking. I'd got mixed up with someone who was nothing to do with me, in a fairytale whose rules I wasn't a party to. 'You must be able to wait six months,' she'd said. 'If you can manage to wait that long, we can see each other again . . .'

The moment they noticed me I must have looked rather like the grate Cinderella was cleaning out when the prince arrived to save her from the yoke of her step-mother and two ugly sisters. I say *they* noticed me, but actually it wasn't the Orange Girl who picked me out

83

first, but the bearded man. (Can you understand any of this, Georg? I couldn't.) He clutched the Orange Girl's arm, pointed to me and said in such a loud and distinct voice that the whole plaza could hear: 'Jan Olav!' I could tell by his accent that he was Danish. I'd never met him in my life.

What happened next only lasted a brief second, but you must try to picture it. The Orange Girl caught sight of me under the orange tree. For an instant or two she stood stock still by a large fountain in the middle of the plaza and stared at me, but she was struck so motionless that after the first second it looked as if she'd been in that same attitude for a full hour or two and could no longer break out of it. But then she did move. Sleeping Beauty had slept for a hundred years, but now she had come back to life again as if it was only a split second since she'd fallen asleep. She came running over to me, put an arm round my neck and simply repeated what the Dane had said: 'Jan Olav!'

Then it was the Dane's turn, Georg. He came sauntering over to the table where I was sitting, proffered me a strong hand and said in a friendly tone: 'It's great to meet you in the flesh, Jan Olav!' The Orange Girl had already taken a chair at the table, and the Dane laid a hand on her shoulder and said: 'Well, it looks as if I'm in the way here.' And with those words he gave way, backed out, turned on his heel and slouched away across the plaza the same way he'd come. And he was gone. We were rid of him. The guardian angels were on my side.

She sat opposite me across the table. She had laid both her hands in mine. She was smiling warmly, if slightly flustered, but warmly.

'You didn't manage it,' she said. 'You didn't manage to wait for me!'

'No,' I admitted. 'Because now my heart's bleeding with sorrow.'

I looked at her; she was still smiling. I tried to smile too, but couldn't quite manage it.

'And so I've lost the wager,' I added.

She thought for a bit, then said: 'In life we sometimes need to be able to *yearn* a little. I wrote to you. I tried to give you strength to yearn a little more.'

I could feel my shoulders heaving. 'And so I've lost,' I said again.

'Well, you've been bad,' she said with an uncertain smile. 'But the situation isn't irretrievable.'

'How?'

'It's just as before. It's a matter of how patient you are.'

'I don't understand any of it,' I said.

She squeezed my hands tenderly. 'What don't you understand, Jan Olav?' was all she said, whispering the words, sighing them out.

'The rules,' I said. 'I don't understand the rules.'

And thus began our long conversation.

Georg! I don't need to report everything we said to each other that evening and night, and I wouldn't even be able to remember it all. I know, too, that you'll have a number of questions that you probably want answering as soon as possible.

One of the first things I wanted explained was how the Orange Girl knew my name and where my parents lived. It touched on the picture postcard from Seville, and that was, after all, the last thing that had happened. I sat looking enquiringly at her, and then she said gently: 'Jan Olav . . . don't you remember me, really?'

I studied her. I tried to look at her as if I'd met her for the very first time. I didn't just look into the dark eyes and examine the knowing face; I let my glance fall on her naked shoulders – she let me do this – and I glimpsed down at her thin dress. But it was no easy task trying to remember her out of the context of those few meetings we'd had before Christmas. If I'd met the Orange Girl earlier in my life, it was quite impossible to recall now, for as I sat there then I was incapable of concentrating on anything but her infinite beauty. She had been created by God, I thought, or perhaps it had been Pygmalion, the legendary Greek hero who had hewn his ideal woman out of marble, and then the goddess of love had taken pity on him and brought his sculpture to life. The last time I'd seen the Orange Girl she'd been wearing a black winter coat, but now she was so thinly dressed it made me embarrassed, I felt I was getting *too* close to her, almost. But even so I couldn't recollect her, or perhaps it was because of that.

'Can't you try to remember me?' she repeated. 'I so want you to.'

'Can you give me a clue?' I entreated.

'Humleveien, you idiot!'

Humleveien. The road I'd grown up in. The road I'd been born in. The road I'd lived in all my life. I'd been in Adamstuen for less than six months.

'Or Irisveien,' she said.

That was a road in the same neighbourhood. Humleveien branched off Irisveien.

'Well, Kløverveien, then!'

Another road in the area. When I was small I often played on a large piece of waste ground between the detached houses of Kløverveien. It was a large hummock with bushes and trees. I think there was a sand-pit there too, and a seesaw. A few years ago they put some benches there.

I looked at the Orange Girl again. Then a shock went through my body. It must have been something like waking up from deep hypnosis. I gripped her hands tightly, tightly. I was about to burst into tears. Then I said it. 'Veronika!' I explained.

She beamed. But I'm wondering if she didn't wipe a tear from the corner of her eye as well.

I sat there looking into her eyes, and now my gaze didn't waver. Nothing could hold me back now, I banished all bashfulness. Suddenly, I had the courage to bare my soul to her. I had the courage to abandon myself to the Orange Girl without reservation. It felt like a huge relief.

Perhaps there is no intimacy to compare with two gazes that meet with firmness and determination and simply won't relinquish each other.

The girl with the brown eyes had lived in Irisveien. We had been together almost every day since we'd learnt to walk, and certainly since we'd learnt to talk. We started in the same class at school, but after Christmas that year Veronika and her parents had left the city. We were seven years old at the time. It was only twelve or thirteen years ago. But after that we'd never seen each other again.

We two were always playing together on the big knoll in Kløverveien amongst bushes, flowers and trees.

It was there that we'd lived our squirrels' lives together – complete squirrels' lives. Even if Veronika hadn't left Irisveien when she did, that carefree childhood would soon have come to an end. There were already whispers in the playground that I preferred playing with girls.

I remembered a song one of us had heard at home, and which we always sang when we were out playing: *I know of a little boy, who'd like to play with a little girl. All day long there'd be such joy, in our very own dream world* . . .

'But you didn't recognise me,' she was saying. I couldn't ignore her tone of disappointment, it was verging on sulkiness. Suddenly it was a seven-year-old I was talking to and not a grown woman of twenty.

I had to look at her again. I thought her red dress was so delectably pretty and enticing. I could just see her body breathing under the dress: it rose and fell, rose and fell, like sea breakers on a beautiful beach, and the beach was her dress.

I glanced into the air. Then I caught sight of a yellow butterfly between the leaves of an orange tree. It wasn't the first one I'd seen that day.

So I pointed up at it and said: 'How can I recognise a little caterpillar long after it's turned into a butterfly?'

'Jan Olav!' she said sternly. Not a word more was said about her metamorphosis from childhood to womanhood.

I still had many unanswered questions. My acquaintance with the Orange Girl had almost driven me crazy, had certainly shaken my existence to its core. I went straight to it.

'We met each other in Oslo. We met three times, and I've thought of practically nothing else ever since. Then you just vanished, flew away. It was harder to keep hold of you than to catch a butterfly with bare hands. But why six months before we could see each other again?'

It was because she had to go to Seville, naturally. I'd realised that much. But why was it so vital for her to spend six months in Spain? Was it on account of the Dane perhaps?

I'm sure you can guess her answer to that, Georg. I couldn't, but then you've seen what your mother is passionate about. All the time I've been writing this long letter to you, I've been wondering if the big painting of orange trees is still hanging in the lobby. Her usual line – at the time of writing – is that she's grown out of that picture, but I hope for your sake that she hasn't given it way or stored it up in the attic. If she has, I think you should ask about it.

'I'd got a place at an art school,' she said, 'or at a school of painting to be more accurate. I was determined to complete the course. It was important to me.'

'School of painting?' I said. I was astounded. 'But why couldn't you say anything about it on Christmas Eve?'

When she didn't answer immediately, I went on: 'Do you remember how it snowed? Do you remember me stroking your hair? Do you remember how the church bells suddenly rang out as the taxi arrived? Then you'd gone!'

'I remember everything,' she said. 'I remember it like a film. I remember it like the opening scenes in a very . . . romantic film.'

'So I can't understand why you had to be so secretive,' I interjected.

A serious look stole over her face. 'I think I began to like you even when we bumped into each other on the

Frogner tram,' she said. 'Like you again, you might say, but now in a totally new way. Then we met a few times subsequently. But I thought we could stand being away from each other for six months. I thought that maybe we needed it. We'd been so close as children. But we aren't children any more. Maybe now we needed to yearn for one another a little. I mean, so that we wouldn't just begin playing together out of old habit. I wanted you to discover me all over again. I wanted you to recognise me, the way I'd recognised you. That was why I didn't let on who I was.'

I can't recall just what reply I made to this, and I can't recollect everything the Orange Girl said either, but gradually, as our conversation proceeded, we began jumping from one subject to another or, more often, from one episode to another.

'And your Danish friend?' I asked when the opportunity arose. It felt as if I was coaxing something out of her. It was silly. I felt I was being petty.

She was terse, almost severe. 'He's called Mogens. He's on the painting course too. He's very good. It's nice there's another Scandinavian here.'

My head was reeling. 'But how did he know my name?' I queried.

I'm trying to think if she blushed at this, but I'm not sure, it was difficult to tell because of the red dress perhaps, and by then it was almost completely dark, only a couple of wrought iron lanterns cast a golden sheen across the empty plaza. We had ordered a bottle of red Ribera del Duero wine and sat holding our glasses.

'I've painted a portrait of you,' she said. 'Just from memory, but it's a good likeness. Mogens likes it. You can see it sometime. It's just called *Jan Olav*.'

So it was Veronika who'd painted her face on the postcard. I didn't need to ask. But there was something else troubling me. 'So it wasn't Mogens in the white Toyota?' I enquired.

She laughed. It was as if she was trying to change the subject. 'You didn't imagine that I didn't see you that time at the fuit market? I was only there because of you.'

I didn't understand what she meant. She seemed to be talking in riddles. But she went on: 'First we met on the Frogner tram. Then I sniffed around town for a while and discovered your favourite café. One day I went in – I'd never been there before – after I'd bought a book about the Spanish painter Velázquez. I sat there just turning the pages. I was waiting.'

'For me?'

I knew it was a stupid question. Her reply sounded close to irritation: 'Surely you don't think you're the only one searching? I'm part of this story, too. I'm not just some butterfly for you to catch.'

I didn't dare go deeper into such questions, it was too dangerous at the moment. I simply said: 'But what about Youngstorget?'

'Don't be so childish, Jan Olav. I've already told you. Where is Jan Olav? I wondered. And where would he try to find me, that is if he really *wants* to find me, after twice meeting me with a large bag of oranges? I couldn't be quite certain of it, but I thought you might look for me in the city's biggest fruit market. I went there lots of times looking for you. But I went to other places as well. I went to Kløverveien and I went to Humleveien. Once I went and saw your parents. I regretted it the moment they opened the door, but what was done was done. I said something to them about it being my childhood home and old stamping grounds. And I didn't need to tell *them* my name, for your information. They recognised me immediately. They invited me in, but I said I was in a bit of a hurry. I said I'd got a place at a school of painting in Seville.'

I didn't know whether to believe her. 'They haven't said a word about it to me,' I said.

She sat there wreathed in an enigmatic smile. I thought she looked a bit like the Mona Lisa, but perhaps that was because at the back of my mind was the fact that she went to an art school. 'I asked them not to tell you I'd been there,' she said. 'I was forced to invent a sort of explanation for why you oughtn't to know.'

I was dumbstruck. Only a few days before I'd had to show Mum and Dad the postcard from Seville. I'd come rushing in and said I was going to get married. Only now did I see why they'd been so quick to lend me money for the plane ticket. They hadn't once questioned the advisability of travelling to Seville in the middle of the semester merely to try to meet a girl I'd bumped into a couple of times in Oslo.

'It's not always easy to find a particular person in a large city, at least not if what you want to do is meet them as if by chance,' the Orange Girl continued. 'And sometimes that's exactly what you do want to do. I was going on the painting course, and I didn't want to get tied up with someone just before I left. But if two people do almost nothing except search for one another, it's hardly surprising if they run across each other by chance.'

I changed the subject, or perhaps I should say the location.

'Had you been to the Christmas service at the cathedral before?' I asked.

She shook her head. 'No, never. And you?'

I shook my head as well.

She said: 'Well, yes, I had been to the 2 p.m. service as well. Afterwards I walked the streets waiting for the next one. You just *had* to turn up to that. It was Christmas, and I would soon be going abroad.'

I seem to remember we sat there for a long time without speaking. But there was a connecting thread I had to return to. 'So it wasn't Mogens in the Toyota?'

'No,' she said.

'Who was it then?'

She hesitated a fraction before answering. 'No one,' she said.

'No one?' I queried.

'He was a sort of ex-boyfriend. We were in the same class at sixth-form college.'

I think I smiled. Even so she said: 'We can't own each other's pasts, Jan Olav. The question is whether we have a future together.'

Just then I came out with something horribly corny, and maybe that was because I didn't dare hope that the Orange Girl and I might have a future together. I said: 'To be two or not to be two, that is the question.'

I think she thought it was a bit pathetic as well. To cover it up I began to talk about something completely different. 'But all those oranges?' I exclaimed, 'What were you going to do with them? Yes, what were you going to do with all those oranges?'

She had a good laugh. 'Yes, I'm sure you puzzled long and hard about that. It was because of the oranges that I lured you to Youngstorget fruit market. It was because of them you began talking about a skiing expedition across Greenland. With an eight-dog team and ten kilos of oranges.'

I saw no reason to deny it. But I asked again: 'What did you *want* with all those oranges?'

At this she looked into my eyes, much as she'd done in the café in Oslo. Then quite slowly she said, 'I was going to paint them.'

Paint them? I was flabbergasted. 'All of them?'

She nodded gracefully, then she said, 'I had to practise painting oranges before I went to art school in Seville.'

'But so many?'

'Yes, I had to paint lots of oranges. That was what I was practising.'

I shook my head despairingly. Was she making a fool of me? 'But couldn't you have bought one orange, and then tried to paint it several times?'

She tilted her head to one side and said in a voice full of resignation. 'I think you and I may have a lot to talk about in the future, because I believe you're probably blind in one eye.'

'Which one?'

'No two oranges are alike, Jan Olav. Even two blades of grass aren't alike. That's the reason you're here now.'

I felt foolish. I couldn't understand what she was driving at. 'Because no two oranges are the same?'

'You didn't come all that way to Seville because you wanted to meet "a woman". If you did, you'll have gone to a whole lot of unnecessary trouble because Europe is full of women. You came to meet me. And there's only one of me. I didn't send a card from Seville to "a man" in Oslo. I sent it to you. I asked you to stay true to me. I asked you to trust me a little.'

We sat there talking until long after the café had closed. When at last we rose, she pulled me close to the

94

trunk of the orange tree whose canopy we'd been sitting under – or was it me who pulled her, I can't quite remember. But it was she who said, 'You can kiss me now, Jan Olav. Because now I've caught you at last.'

I put my hands on her shoulders and kissed her lightly on the mouth. She said, 'No, you must kiss me properly! And you must hold me in your arms.'

I did as the Orange Girl had bidden me. It was she who laid down the rules. She tasted of vanilla. Her hair smelt fresh as citrus.

I had the decided feeling that two spry squirrels were clambering about high in the orange tree's crown. I wasn't sure what game they were playing, but at any rate it was something they were wildly engrossed in.

I won't say a lot more about that evening, Georg, I think I should spare you that. But you'll have to listen to how the night itself ended.

I didn't manage to get to my guest house before midnight. But the Orange Girl rented a small room and kitchenette from an old lady. On the walls hung several watercolours of orange flowers and orange trees. And in one corner of the room stood a large oil painting of me. I made no comment about that picture, and neither did she. It would have been going too deeply into the very magic of this fairytale. Not everything was to be put into words. Those were the rules. But I thought she'd painted me with eyes that were much too large and far too blue. It was as if she had invested those eyes with every bit of personality I had.

I lay there telling Veronika various long tales full of amusing details until far into the night. I told of a clergyman's sickly daughter with four sisters and two brothers, and a disobedient labrador. I told the long, eventful tale of a skiing expedition across Greenland in its entirety, including the eight-dog sledge team and the ten kilos of oranges. I told of the resilient girl who was a UN undercover agent in the Inspectorate of Oranges, waging a brave and lonely battle against a dangerous, new orange virus. I told all I knew of a girl who worked at a nursery school and had to go to the market each day to buy thirty-six absolutely identical oranges. I disclosed details about a young lady who was making orange mousse for a hundred students at the School of Management. I related the entire life story of the nineteen-year-old girl who was married to one of the students and had already had a daughter by him – despite his repulsiveness in the eyes of many. And I told of the courageous and self-sacrificing girl who, in secret, smuggled food and medicines to poor children in Africa.

The Orange Girl chipped in by recounting some shared reminiscences from our childhood in Humleveien and Irisveien. Personally, I'd forgotten nearly everything, but I remembered a little of it while she was speaking.

When we awoke the sun stood high in the sky. She was the first to stir, and I'll never forget what it felt like to be woken by her. I could no longer tell what was imagination and what was reality; perhaps the borderline between them didn't exist any more. All I knew was that I was no longer wandering about looking for the Orange Girl. Now I had found her.

I had, too. Now I knew who the Orange Girl was, and I should have guessed it long before I found out that her name was Veronika . . .

When I'd read to about here, Mum knocked on my door

again. 'It's ten thirty, Georg. We've laid the table. Have you got much more to read?' she asked.

In a slightly declamatory voice I said: 'Dear little Orange Girl. I've been thinking of you. Can you wait a little longer?'

I couldn't see her on the other side of the door. But I heard her go quite still. 'In life we must sometimes be able to *yearn* a little,' I said.

When no answer came, I said, 'I know of a little boy . . .'

It was still completely quiet on the other side of the door. But then I heard Mum come right up close to it. Softly, she sang into the door frame, '. . . who'd like to play with a little girl . . .'

She couldn't manage any more of the song, as just then she began to cry. She cried in whispers.

'All day long there'd be such joy, in our very own dream world . . .' I whispered back.

She sighed and then said weepily, 'Is that really . . . what he's writing about?'

'Wrote,' I said.

She made no answer, but I could tell from the door handle that she was leaning against the door.

'I'll come soon, Mum,' I whispered. 'There's only fifteen more pages.'

She said nothing to that, either. Perhaps she wasn't able to. I couldn't tell what havoc I might have wreaked out there.

Poor Jørgen, I thought. For once in his life he'd have to put up with playing second fiddle. Miriam was sleeping. Now it was Dad and Mum and me who were doing the talking. Once we'd been a little family in Humleveien. And then, in the living room there was Grandma and Grandpa, and they'd originally built this house. Jørgen was only a visitor.

I thought carefully about everything I'd read. Something important had already been answered. Dad hadn't tried to take me for a ride. He hadn't invented a fairytale about an Orange Girl. Perhaps he hadn't revealed everything. But everything he'd said had been true.

I couldn't remember seeing a painting of orange trees in the lobby. I couldn't remember a single picture of oranges. I'd only seen all the other pictures Mum had painted. I'd seen her watercolours of the lilacs and cherries in our own garden.

There were several things of this sort I had to talk to her about, or go up to the attic and take a look myself. But I knew that Mum had lived in Irisveien when she was little. I'd once been to the yellow-painted house to hand in a letter that had been delivered to our mailbox.

Perhaps I'd learn more about the orange paintings when I read on. Then there was another important thing: would Dad say more about the Hubble Space Telescope?

The Hubble Space Telescope was named after the astronomer Edwin Powell Hubble. He was the one who proved that the universe is expanding. First he discovered that the Andromeda Halo wasn't merely a cloud of dust particles and gas in our own galaxy, but that it was a completely independent galaxy outside the Milky Way. The discovery that the Milky Way is merely one of many galaxies revolutionised astronomers' notions of space.

Hubble's most important discovery came in 1929 when he was able to show that the further away a galaxy is from the Milky Way, the faster it appears to be moving. This discovery is the very foundation of what is known as the Big

Bang theory. According to this theory, which is accepted by almost all astronomers today, the universe was created after a huge explosion about 12–14 billion years ago. That's a long time ago, a very long time ago.

If the entire history of the universe was explained within the time-frame of a single day, the Earth wouldn't have been formed until late in the afternoon. The dinosaurs would have arrived a few minutes before midnight. And human beings would only have existed for the final two seconds.

Are you still there, Georg? I've sat down at my computer again after walking you to nursery school. It's Monday.

You were a bit grizzly today. I took your temperature, but it wasn't raised. I looked into your throat and ears, too, and felt some of your glands but I found nothing. I think you've just got a bit of a cold, and perhaps you're a little exhausted after the weekend.

I was almost hoping there might be something mildly wrong with you so that you could stay at home with me all day. But, then, I have this writing to do.

We were at Fjellstølen again this weekend. Early on Saturday morning Mum went off for a long walk carrying an old milk can and came back with four kilos of cloudberries. You were a bit grumpy about that, Georg. You insisted on going berrying in the mountains too, and during the afternoon you managed to pick half a kilo of crowberries all by yourself. We kept an eye on you from the cabin, of course. Then Mum had to make crowberry jelly. We had it on Sunday. I think you found it a bit sour, but you had to taste it as you were the one who'd gathered the berries.

We've seen lots of lemmings this summer, and we let

you draw a lemming in the hut book with yellow and black crayons. It was good; with a little imagination it really is possible to see that the animal you drew is a lemming. It's just that you made its tail far too long. So, for safety's sake Mum wrote 'LEMMING' under the drawing. Then she wrote 'Georg 1/9/1990'.

Perhaps the cabin book is still there? Is it, Georg?

I sat there almost all that evening reading through the cabin book from beginning to end. It was after you'd gone to bed. I went through it several times. As soon as I'd read the final entry – and gazed at your drawing once again – I went back to the beginning. I assumed it would be our last visit to the cabin before Christmas.

Finally, Veronika came and snatched the book out of my hands. She put it high up on the bookshelf, although it usually sits on the mantelpiece.

'Now we'll have a little drink,' was all she said.

But to return to Spain.

I stayed with Veronika in Seville for a couple of days. Then it was time to go home, and both Veronika and her landlady agreed. I'd have to try to wait almost three more months before she'd finished her painting course. But now I had learnt to yearn. I'd learnt to trust the Orange Girl.

Of course I had to ask if she was still going to honour her old promise about us being together every day for the following six months. I could no longer take it as read because I hadn't managed to abide by the rules myself. She thought for a long time before answering. I think she was trying to find a witty rejoinder. Then with a smile she said, 'Perhaps it'll be enough if I deduct the two days you've already had in advance here.'

When she accompanied me to the airport bus, we saw a white dove lying dead in the gutter. Veronika stopped and shivered. I thought it odd that it should have such an effect on her. But then she turned towards me, put her head on my chest and cried. Then I began to cry too. We were so young. We were caught up in the midst of a fairytale. A dead dove shouldn't have been lying in the gutter. Not a white one, anyway. Those were the rules. We wept. That white dove was an ill omen.

Back in Oslo I concentrated on my studies. I had a lot to catch up on as I'd missed several important lectures during the previous week, and some work was outstanding owing to all the skiing trips and urban ramblings I'd been going on during the past few months. But I saved a lot of time now that I didn't have to traipse round town looking for a mysterious Orange Girl. Nor did I need to expend a lot of effort getting a girlfriend. Many of my fellow students spent a lot of time on that sort of thing.

I would still sometimes start when I caught sight of a woman's black coat, or a red summer dress when the weather got warmer. Each time I saw an orange I thought of Veronika. When I was out shopping, the orange display could send me into a reverie. I'd got much better at seeing that no two oranges were identical. I could stand there calmly scrutinising them. And if I was buying oranges myself, I took plenty of time and always selected the very finest. Sometimes I would squeeze the juice from the oranges, and on one occasion when we were playing bridge at the flat, I made orange mousse which I served up to Gunnar and some other friends.

Gunnar was a second-year political science student, and

he was the real cook of the two of us. He was always dishing up beef or cod dishes. And although he never looked for any return, it was nice to be able to surprise him with an orange mousse. I put a lot of soul into that pudding. Mum, your Grandma, helped me find a recipe in an old cookery book. She even offered to make orange mousse for me. She couldn't know that the whole idea was that I should make it myself. I don't think she had the slightest inkling that this project of mine had anything to do with Veronika.

Then she returned home to Norway, Georg. In mid-July she came back from Seville. I went to Fornebu airport to meet her. Many were the witnesses to our great reunion when she emerged from Customs with two large suitcases and a big portfolio of paintings and drawings. We stood for about half a minute just looking at each other first, perhaps to demonstrate that we had sufficient strength of character to wait a few more seconds for one another. But then we melted into an ardent embrace, very ardent in fact, even for an airport. An old lady who was passing by had something to say about it. 'You should be ashamed of yourselves!' she barked. We just laughed. We had nothing to be ashamed of. We'd waited for each other for six months.

We hadn't even left the Arrivals hall before Veronika had to open her portfolio and show me what she'd done. She flipped quickly past the portrait of *Jan Olav*, although I caught a glimpse of it and again noted the intense blueness that radiated from the eyes in the picture. I couldn't say anything about it, but Veronika had lots of amusing comments about the other pictures. She talked non-stop. She made no attempt to conceal how proud she was of the pictures she showed me. She didn't hide the fact that she had *learnt* something during the previous six months.

We spent the rest of the summer lost in romance. We went out to the islands in Oslofjord, we travelled up country, we visited museums and art exhibitions, we passed many sated summer evenings strolling in the villa-lined suburbs of Tåsen.

You should have seen her! You should have seen the way she moved through the city. You should have seen how she carried herself at exhibitions. And you should have heard the way she laughed. My laughter could be uproarious, too. Laughter is one of the most infectious things I know.

We used the pronoun 'we' more and more often. It's a strange word. Tomorrow I'm going to do this or that, we say. Or you ask what the other person, what 'you', are going to do. This isn't hard to understand. But suddenly the word 'we' emerges and with the greatest spontaneity. 'Shall we take a boat out to the islands and go swimming?' 'Or shall we just stay at home and read?' 'Did we enjoy that play?' And then one day, 'We're happy!'

When we use the 'we' pronoun we place two people behind a joint action almost as if they form a composite being. Many languages have a special pronoun to use about two – and only two – people. This pronoun is called *dual*, or something that is shared by two. I think it's a useful concept, because there are times when subjects are neither single nor many. You are 'we two', and a 'we two' as if that 'we' cannot be split. When this pronoun suddenly makes its appearance, fairytale rules come into play, as if with the wave of a wand. 'We'll make dinner.' 'We'll open a bottle of wine.' 'We'll go to bed.' Talking like that is almost shameless, isn't it? At any rate, it's quite different to saying: you must take the bus home now, because I want to get some sleep.

When we use the *dual*, certain totally new rules come into play. 'We'll go for a walk!' It's so simple, Georg, just five words, and yet they describe a chain of events so pregnant with meaning that they go deep into the lives of two people on earth. And in this context energy-saving isn't even limited to words. 'We'll shower!' Veronika said. 'We'll eat!' 'We'll go to bed!' You don't need more than one shower-head when that form is used. You don't need more than one kitchen and one bed.

As far as I was concerned this new pronoun came as quite a shock. 'We' – it was as if something had come full circle. It was as if the whole world had coalesced into a higher unity.

Youth, Georg, youthful gaiety!

And I remember one warm August evening when we sat looking out across the fjord from the Bygdøy penin-sula. I don't quite know where I got it from, but I suddenly blurted out: 'We're only in this world once.'

'We're here now,' said Veronika, as if she thought we ought to remind ourselves of the fact.

But I felt she was brushing off what I was trying to express, because then I said: 'I think of evenings like this that I'll no more be able to know . . .' I knew that Veronika remembered that line from one of Olaf Bull's poems. It was a poem we had once read together.

Suddenly Veronika turned to me and pinched my ear with her fingers. 'But then at least you've been here. Lucky you!' she said.

When autumn arrived Veronika started at art school and I

continued my medical training. After the first preliminary courses it became more and more interesting. We spent as much time together as possible in the afternoons and evenings, and we made sure that we at least *saw* each other every day. But the Orange Girl really did deduct the two full days that I owed her. I think she did it mainly to tease me, but perhaps it was also to set an example. We still had to abide by the rules; the fairytale wasn't over, it had only just begun. More and more fairytale grew up around us, and so there were ever more rules to obey. You remember what I said about these rules? That they're important things you must either do or not do, but which you don't necessarily have to understand. You don't even need to talk about them.

Veronika had managed to find a bedsit and kitchenette in Oslo too, which she rented from another old lady. Her rent was mowing the lawn in summer, shovelling snow in winter and doing her landlady's shopping every few days, including a weekly bottle of port from the off-licence. But the old lady, whose name was Mrs Mowinckel, didn't mind me doing these chores now and again. This was good, as it gradually led her to accepting my occasional overnight stays in the cramped lodgings. I'd already paid my rent.

When Christmas arrived, we went to the service at the cathedral again – we thought we owed each other that much. Veronika was wearing the same black coat, and her hair was decorated with the same marvellous silver hair-clip. Now I'd become part of the fairytale myself, part of the same unfathomable mystery. This year we shared the same pew of course, and I didn't need to worry about which way the men in church were looking. They were welcome to look at Veronika, and some did. I felt proud. Veronika was radiant and she was happy. I was happy too, of course. Perhaps she felt a little pride as well.

After the service we took exactly the same route as the year before. We had talked about it. We were already conscious of tradition. Almost without speaking we walked together up to the Palace park. We hadn't intended the silence; that just happened.

We stood holding each other at exactly the same spot where she'd jumped into the taxi the year before, for we were going our separate ways again this Christmas. Veronika was to meet her father at an elderly aunt's in Skillebekk, and from there they would drive to Asker where her parents lived. I was to spend my Christmas in Humleveien again, together with Mum and Dad and Uncle Einar.

The scene was just as it had been the year before. We would take leave of each other here in Wergelandsveien as soon as an empty taxi arrived that Veronika could jump into. But what would happen after the taxi came? Would the fairytale be over? Would the magic spell suddenly be broken? We hadn't talked about that. We'd seen each other every day for the past six months, apart from the cruel punishment of those two days. The Orange Girl had kept her solemn promise. But what were the rules for the coming year?

It was colder this Christmas and Veronika was shivering. I put my arms around her and rubbed her back. Then I told her that Gunnar was going to move out of the small flat we shared in the New Year. He was going to continue his studies in Bergen, I said. I told her I had to find another student to share with.

I was such a coward, Georg. I think she thought so

too. She was almost cross. Gunnar was going to move out? And I had to find a new student for the flat? Had I really been planning this without consulting her? She was close to anger. I began to fear that we might part on bad terms that Christmas. Then she said: 'But I can move in with you. I mean, you and I can live together. We can, can't we, Jan Olav?'

It was exactly what I'd been wanting. But I was less daring than she was. I was worried about breaking the rules.

She lit up like an orange tree on the Plaza de la Alianza when we quickly agreed that she could move to Adamstuen in early January. In the coming year we wouldn't just be together every single day, but every single night as well. Those were the new rules.

But then an anxious look stole across her face, perhaps indicating some kind of doubt, I thought, perhaps she was going to impose a condition after all. Or was she hoping for something that she found hard to talk about? 'What's the matter, Veronika?' I whispered. I could read her now.

'Gunnar's room will be empty, then,' she said.

I nodded, not understanding why she was mentioning it again. I'd said that Gunnar was moving out.

'Well, we won't be sleeping in separate rooms!' she said.

'Of course not,' I said, still not grasping what she was driving at.

Now she had no doubts left. She just sang right out: 'In that case, perhaps I could use Gunnar's room as a studio?' She gave me a fleeting glance to see how I was reacting. I simply laid my hand on the silver hair-clip at her neck and said that I'd feel terribly proud to be living with an artist.

Within the next minute or two her taxi arrived. She hailed it. She got into the car, and this year she turned and waved excitedly to me with both hands. To think that it was only one year on!

I didn't need to look round for a cast-off glass slipper when the taxi had gone. Our fairytale contained no more conditions. We were no longer dependent on some fussy fairy's opaque rules about what was permitted and what wasn't. Now happiness was ours.

But what is a person, Georg? How much is a person worth? Are we nothing but dust that is whipped up and spread to the winds?

As I write these lines, the Hubble Space Telescope is in its orbit round the earth. It has been out there for more than four months now, and already, since late May it has managed to send us many valuable pictures of the universe, of that huge waste that we are ultimately descended from. But they also quickly discovered that the telescope has a serious manufacturing fault. There's already talk of sending up a space shuttle with a crew who can repair this flaw, and so give us an even better under-standing of space.

Do you know how things have gone with the Hubble Space Telescope? Was it ever repaired?

Sometimes I think of the space telescope as the Eye of the Universe. For the eye that can see the entire universe has a certain right to be called the Eye of the Universe. Do you understand what I mean by that? It is the universe itself that has produced this unbelievable instrument. The Hubble Space Telescope is a cosmic sensory organ.

What *is* this great fairytale we live in and which each

of us is only permitted to experience for such a short time? Maybe the space telescope will help us to understand more of the nature of this fairytale one day. Perhaps out there, behind the galaxies, lies the answer to what a human being is.

I believe I've used the word 'riddle' many times in this letter. Attempting to understand the universe is perhaps comparable to doing a great jigsaw puzzle. Although possibly it's as much a mental or *intellectual* riddle, and we may have the answer to it within us. We are here, after all. We are the universe.

Perhaps we aren't fully developed. The physical development of human beings necessarily had to precede the psychological. Perhaps the physical nature of the universe is merely a necessary external material for its own self-awareness.

I've got a crazy notion: Newton suddenly understood the existence of universal gravity. Fine. Darwin had an almost equally spontaneous insight into biological development on earth. Great. Then Einstein discovered a correlation between mass, energy and the speed of light. Excellent! And, in 1953, Crick and Watson demonstrated how the DNA molecule, the genetic material of plants and animals, was constructed. Brilliant! But then one could also imagine a day – and what a day it would be Georg! – a day when some pensive soul had a flash of inspiration and solved the very mystery of the universe. I think something like that could suddenly happen. (I'd like to be the headline writer of some large daily newspaper that day!)

Do you remember at the start of this letter I said there was something I wanted to ask you about? Your answer will be very important to me. But there is still some more to tell.

The Hubble Space Telescope! There it was again. Now I was completely sure that the big question my dad wanted to ask me must have something to do with space.

I got up from the bed and peered out of the window. It was still snowing hard. But that doesn't matter, I thought. Even if it's overcast on earth, the Hubble Space Telescope can take crystal clear pictures of galaxies many billions of light years away from our own Milky Way. And it does, twenty-four hours a day. It's already supplied us with hundreds of thousands of pictures and investigated more than ten thousand celestial bodies. Each day the Hubble Space Telescope provides us with enough data to fill up a domestic computer.

But why was Dad writing about the space telescope again? I couldn't see how it could have a connection with the Orange Girl. But this was no longer the most important thing. The most important thing of all was that my dad had actually *known* about the Hubble Space Telescope. He had realised how important it was for mankind. He managed to do that before he got sick and died. It was one of the last things he'd been interested in.

The Eye of the Universe! I had never thought of the Hubble Space Telescope in that way. I'd thought of it as mankind's window on the universe. But it really wasn't an exaggeration to call the space telescope the Eye of the Universe.

Perhaps, in its time, the boundless admiration caused by the first Norwegian railway link between Oslo and Eidsvoll was just a bit exaggerated. Norway contains one thousandth of the world's population, and in 1850 the Oslo-Eidsvoll line might have served one ten thousandth of it. With the

Hubble Space Telescope all the citizens of the world can travel round the entire universe. When it was put into orbit round the earth six months before my dad died, the cost of it had risen to 2.2 billion dollars. I've worked out that this is roughly forty cents, or four kroner, per inhabitant of the earth, and I think that's cheap at the price, a ticket allowing travel all over the universe. By way of comparison, a return ticket from Oslo to Eidsvoll now costs about two hundred kroner. That's not particularly cheap, and if there's general agreement, we can organise a complaint to Norwegian Railways. (I'm not intending any disrespect either to Norwegian Railways or the Lilliputian train that once ran from Oslo to Eidsvoll. But I maintain that the Hubble Space Telescope is of more importance for mankind, and perhaps even for the country people living along the railway line. Calling the Hubble Space Telescope the Eye of the Universe is not the least overstatement. My Dad didn't think so anyway, and he didn't even live to see it get new lenses!)

'The Hubble Space Telescope is a cosmic sensory organ,' he wrote. I think I understand what he meant by that. We can perhaps say that it was a small step for mankind to put the Hubble Space Telescope into orbit round the planet, because in 1990 we had powerful telescopes and a space shuttle. But it was a big leap for the universe! Because it's on behalf of the entire universe that man is trying to find an answer to what the universe is. Nothing less! **It has taken the universe almost fifteen billion years to graft on something as fundamental as an eye to see itself by!** (It took me a whole hour to write that sentence, that's why I've put it in bold type.)

I was getting close, I thought. I hurried on with my reading, and soon I was witnessing my own birth. It was spectacular. Not every child is born in the middle of a cocktail party.

But carry on, Dad. I didn't mean to interrupt you. You asked how things stood with the Hubble Space Telescope, and now I've answered that question at least.

From now on I'll be brief. I'll have to be, as time is running out. Tomorrow I've got an important appointment. So Mum will take you to nursery school.

We lived in the little flat in Adamstuen for four years. Veronika finished art school, and continued to paint, as you know, and then gradually started teaching painting at a sixth-form college. As a newly qualified doctor, I was just about to start my stint as a house officer. That meant that I'd have to work in a hospital for two years.

I'm sure you know that Grandma and Grandpa were both born in Tønsberg. It was about this time that they wanted to realise an old dream of theirs and retire to the town. One day they told us they'd bought a small, idyllic house in the Nordbyen district. My brother, your Uncle Einar, had recently run away to sea – I think he was escaping an unhappy love affair. And so it was that Veronika and I took over the large house in Humleveien. We had to take out a big mortgage, but now we knew we had some income.

We did a lot of work on the garden in our first year at Humleveien. Naturally we kept the two apple trees, the pear tree and the cherry tree; all they needed was a little pruning and manure. We kept the old raspberry bushes too, and we hadn't the heart to get rid of the gooseberries, blackcurrants or rhubarb. But we planted lilacs, rhododendrons and hortensia as well. Veronika was in charge. I'd lived with the garden almost all my life. Now it was to be hers. Sometimes on warm days she'd take her easel into the garden and paint whatever was growing there.

Once when we were out picking raspberries we saw a huge bumblebee suddenly take off from a clover flower and fly away at tremendous speed. It struck me that a bumblebee must fly inordinately faster than a jumbo jet, in relation to its body weight. I mentioned this to Veronika and we did a simple calculation. We assumed that a bumblebee weighs twenty grammes and that it flies at a speed of at least ten kilometres per hour. Then there was the jumbo jet. That has a speed of 800 kilometres per hour, in other words eighty times faster than the bumblebee. But eighty times twenty grammes is just 1.8 kilos. Veronika and I agreed that a Boeing 747 weighed a lot more than that. In relation to its body weight, the bumblebee reached speeds that were thousands of times greater than the jumbo jet's. And a Boeing 747 had four jet engines. The bumblebee hadn't. A bumblebee was just powered by winds! We laughed. We laughed because a bumblebee could fly so fast, and we laughed because we lived in Humleveien – Bumblebee Road.

It was Veronika who taught me to look more closely at the finer points of nature, and there were so many of them. We might pick a blue anemone or a violet and stand there studying the little wonder for minutes on end. Wasn't the world just one enormous fairytale?

Today as I write, I feel melancholy thinking of the bumblebee's fleeting seconds of flight that afternoon as we stood out in the garden picking raspberries. We were so transported, Georg, so open and carefree. I hope that you have inherited a mind that is open to such small mysteries. They are no less thought-provoking than the stars and galaxies up above. I think it requires more intelligence to create a bumblebee than a black hole.

For me this has always been a magical world, I've thought so ever since I was quite young, and long before I began to spy on an Orange Girl in the streets of Oslo. I still have the feeling that I've seen something that no one else has seen. It's hard to describe this sensation in simple words, but imagine the world before all this modern fuss about natural laws, evolutionary theory, atoms, DNA molecules, biochemistry and nerve cells − before it began to spin in fact, before it was reduced to being a 'planet' in space, and before the proud human body was divided up into heart, lungs kidneys, liver, brain, blood system, muscles, stomach and intestines. I'm talking about the time when a human being was a human being, a complete and proud *human being*, no more and no less. Then the world was just one sparkling fairytale.

A roe deer suddenly leaps from a thicket, stares intently at you for a second − and is gone. What kind of soul gives motion to that animal? What sort of unfathomable power decorates the earth with flowers in every colour of the rainbow and adorns the night sky with a sumptuous lacework of twinkling stars?

That sort of spontaneous feeling for natural things can be found in folk tales, like the fairytales of the brothers Grimm. Read them, Georg. Read the Icelandic sagas, read the Greek and Norse myths, read the Old Testament.

Look at the world, Georg, look at the world before you've filled yourself with too much physics and chemistry.

At this moment great flocks of wild reindeer are tearing

across the windswept Hardangervidda plateau. On the Île de la Carmargue, between two estuaries of the Rhône, thousands of bright red flamingos are nesting. Seductive herds of nimble gazelles leap magically over the African savannah. Thousands upon thousands of king penguins are chattering away to each other on an icy shore in the Antarctic, and they're not in pain, they enjoy it. But it's not just numbers that count. A lone, contemplative elk lifts its head out of the spruce forest. Last year one of them got lost and wandered right into Humleveien. A terrified lemming dashes about between the boards of the outhouse at Fjellstølen. A plump seal belly-flops from a small island off Tønsberg.

Don't tell me nature isn't a miracle. Don't tell me the world isn't a fairytale. Anyone who hasn't realised that, may never understand until the fairytale is just about to end. Then there is one final chance to tear off the blinkers, a last chance to rub your eyes in amazement, a final opportunity to abandon yourself to the wonder you are bidding farewell to and leaving.

I wonder if you understand what I'm trying to say, Georg. No one has ever taken a tear-choked leave of Euclid's geometry or the periodical system of atoms. No one's eyes become red-rimmed because they will be disconnected from the internet or taken away from their multiplication tables. It is the world you take leave of, life, the fairytale. Then there is the little group of people you are genuinely fond of, you say goodbye to them, too.

Sometimes I wish I'd lived before the invention of multiplication tables, and certainly before modern physics and chemistry, before we thought we knew everything, I mean in THE REALLY MAGICAL WORLD! But that's exactly how the world strikes me at this moment as I sit in front of my computer writing these lines to you. I'm a scientist myself, and I'm not the least dismissive of any of the sciences, but I also possess a mystical, almost animistic view of the world. I've never allowed Newton or Darwin to take the gloss off the mystery of life. (Just use the dictionary to look up any words you don't understand. There's a modern dictionary in the lobby. Well, at least there was when I was writing this, but maybe you won't think it's all that modern now.)

I'll let you into a secret: before I began studying medicine I had two alternative future career plans. Either I wanted to be a writer, someone who celebrates with words this enchanted world we live in. But this is something I've already mentioned. Or I wanted to be a doctor, someone who serves life. For safety's sake I decided to become a doctor first.

I never managed to become a writer. But I did write this letter to you.

To come home from the surgery to an Orange Girl who was out in our own garden painting cherry flowers was like a great consummation of everything I could have dreamt of. Once when I came home, I was so elated at the sight of her in the garden that I lifted her up and carried her all the way up to the bedroom. She laughed, oh, how she laughed! Then I laid her on the bed and ravished her there. I'm not ashamed to let you into that part of our happiness either. Why should I be? It's a connecting thread in this story.

The first thing we decided when we moved in, after several months of renovation, was that we'd stop using birth control. We made that decision the very first night we slept here. From that night on, we'd begun making you.

And after eighteen months at Humleveien you were born, Georg. I was so proud when I held you in my arms for the first time. You were a boy. If you'd been a girl, the name Ranveig would have been almost unavoidable. That was her name, the little daughter of one of the orange girls.

Veronika was tired and pale after the birth, but she was happy. We couldn't have been happier. This was the start of a new chapter with completely new rules.

I'll tell you another secret. One of my student friends was working at the hospital as a doctor. He came to visit us in the delivery room with glasses of champagne for the new mother and father. It wasn't really allowed, in fact it was strictly forbidden. But there was a small curtain that could be pulled across the window giving on to the corridor, and now all three of us toasted the life that you'd begun to live on earth. Of course, you didn't get any champagne yourself, but you were quickly put to Veronika's breast, and she'd had a few small sips of it.

But when the Orange Girl had followed me to the airport bus in Seville that time, we had seen a dead dove lying in the gutter. It was a bad omen. Perhaps because I hadn't followed all the rules of the fairytale.

Do you remember that we went to the cabin this Easter? You were almost three and a half. No, I'm sure you'll have forgotten it all. When you study medicine, you do a little psychology as well. There isn't much you can recall later in life from the time before you were four.

I remember we sat by the cabin wall sharing an orange,

and Veronika recorded it on video, almost as if she felt that something was drawing to a close. Could you ask her if she still has that video, Georg? Perhaps she'll think it's painful to bring it out, but ask her just the same.

After Easter I knew I was seriously ill. Veronika didn't believe it, but I knew. I was good at reading signs. I was good at making diagnoses.

Then I approached a colleague, the same man who'd brought us champagne at the hospital when you were born. First he took some blood tests, then he did what is called a CT scan – it's a kind of x-ray examination – and he agreed with me completely. We shared the same professional opinion.

Now life changed completely. It was a catastrophe for Veronika and me, but we had to try to keep you outside the zone of desolation for as long as possible. Yet again some new rules were hastily put in place. Words like longing, patience and loss became imbued with new meaning now. We couldn't promise to be together every day in the coming years any more. We couldn't promise each other anything at all. Suddenly we'd been left so poor and naked. The heart-warming pronoun 'we' had suffered a nasty rift. We couldn't place any demands on each other now; we couldn't share any expectations of the time that lay before us.

After reading this you know a little about my life. You know who I am. That's something good for me to hold on to.

In a way you know me better than many others, even though we two haven't had a proper talk since you were almost four. I haven't always communicated as openly with others as I have with you in this letter. And so you'll certainly understand how hard it was for me to have to accept these new rules. I knew what was likely to happen, and gradually had to accustom myself to the thought of leaving you and the Orange Girl.

But there is something I must ask you, Georg. It's almost impossible for me to wait any longer. Just let me relate what happened here in Humleveien a few weeks ago.

Veronika is at school in the mornings teaching youngsters to paint oranges. I've told her she's not allowed to stay at home with me the whole day. You and I are the ones who share breakfast together. Then I take you to nursery school, and afterwards I have a few hours to myself when I sit at the computer writing this long letter to you. Often I've got to tiptoe through the room so as not to distrub your train layout. You'd know straight away if anything had been moved.

Sometimes I have to sleep a bit at this time of the day too, not because I'm feeling ill, but because I can't sleep at night; all the thoughts crowd in on me then, that's when they trouble me most. Just as I'm about to drop off I get such a deep glimpse into all the unpleasant mysteries, into that huge and horrible fairytale that has no good fairies, but only black omens, dark spirits and evil elves. So it's better to forget about sleeping at night and drop off on the sofa during the morning when it's light.

I don't find it so hard being awake when I know that you and Veronika are in the house, when I know that you're both lying here sleeping. And anyway I know all I have to do is wake Veronika – and sometimes I do – and she'll sit up with me. On a few occasions we've sat up together all night. We didn't say that much to each other. We just sat together. We made a cup of tea. We ate a slice of bread and cheese. That's what things have come to, Georg. Those are the new rules.

We can sit for hours just holding hands. Once or twice I've peered down at her hand, so gently and lovely, and I've stared at my own hand, perhaps just at one finger, perhaps at a nail. How long will I *have* this finger, I think. Or I've lifted her hand to my lips and kissed it.

I've thought that this hand I'm holding now will be the same one I'll hold in my final moments, perhaps in a hospital bed, and perhaps for hours on end, until I finally cast loose and slip away. We've agreed that that's the way it will be, she's already promised me. It's good to think about. And it's indescribably sad to think about. When I slip away from this universe, it will be a warm and living hand I let go of, the Orange Girl's hand.

Imagine, Georg, if there were a hand to grasp on the other side as well! But I don't believe in another side. I'm almost sure I don't. Everything that exists only lasts until everything is ended. But the last thing a human being clutches is often a hand.

I said that one of the most infectious things I know is laughter. But sorrow can also be contagious. Fear is different. It isn't as communicable as laughter or sadness, and a good thing too. Fear is almost entirely a lonely thing.

I'm scared. Georg. I'm scared about being thrust out of this world. I'm scared of evenings like this that I'll no longer be able to know.

But one night you woke up, that was what I was about to say. I was sitting in the conservatory, and suddenly I saw you come padding out of your room and into the living room. You rubbed your eyes and looked round.

Normally you'd simply have gone upstairs to our bedroom, but this time you just stood in the living room, possibly because you saw that all the lights were on. I walked into the living room from the conservatory and picked you up. You said you couldn't sleep. Maybe you said that because you'd heard Mum and me talking occasionally about the way Dad couldn't sleep.

I have to admit to a pang of instant and incalculable joy when you woke up, that you came out to Daddy when he needed you most. And so I did nothing to help you back to sleep again.

I had such a need to talk to you about everything, but I knew I couldn't, you were far too young. Even so, you were old enough to comfort me. If you could only keep awake, I wanted to sit with you for a few hours that night. It was one of those nights I might have woken Veronika. Now she could sleep in peace.

I knew there was a brilliant starry sky outside, I'd seen it from the conservatory. It was the second half of August, and possibly you'd never looked at a starry sky before, not during the light summer nights that lay behind us anyway, and the previous year you'd have been too young. I dressed you in a warm jumper and woollen trousers, put on an outdoor jacket myself and we went out and sat on the patio, you and I. I'd turned off the lights inside, and now I switched the outside ones off as well.

First I pointed up at the silver-thin moon. It hung low in the eastern sky. Its sickle pointed to the right, so it was on the wane. I explained that to you.

You sat on my lap imbibing all the security that enveloped you. I drank in all the assurance that flowed from you as well. Then I began to point out all the stars and planets high up in the vault of the sky. I wanted so much to tell you everything, everything about the great fairytale we were a part of, the enormous jigsaw of which you and I were just a few tiny pieces. That fairytale, too, had certain laws and rules which we couldn't understand, which we could like or dislike, but which we nevertheless had to submit to.

I knew that soon I might be leaving you, but I couldn't tell you that. I knew that I was probably on my way out of that great fairytale which you and I now sat looking at, but I couldn't confide that to you. Instead, I began to tell you about the stars, at first in a way you could understand but, as I warmed to the subject, I was soon talking freely about space as if you'd been a grown-up son.

And you let me talk, Georg. You enjoyed listening to me talking, even though you weren't able to understand all the riddles I was touching on. Maybe you understood a bit more of what I was saying than I imagined. You certainly didn't interrupt, or fall asleep. It was as if you realised that on this night you couldn't let me down. Perhaps you sensed that it wasn't really me sitting up with you. It was you sitting up with me. You were Daddy-sitting.

I explained that it was night because the earth had turned on its own axis and now had its back pointing towards the sun. Only when the sun is actually rising or setting can we see that the sphere of the earth is turning, I said. Maybe you understood that, even though we sometimes sang a lullaby that began: *The sun is closing his eyes now, and soon I'll do so too . . .* Do you remember that?

I pointed up at Venus and told you that that star was a

planet orbiting the sun just like the earth did. At that time of year we could see Venus low in the sky to the east because the sun was shining on it in just the same way as it shines on earth. Then I told you a secret. I said that every time I looked up at that planet I thought of Veronika, because 'Venus' was an old word for love.

But almost all the other shining points of light we could see in the sky were proper stars, I went on to explain, and they shone by themselves like the sun, since each tiny little star in the sky was a fiery sun. Do you know what your response to that was? You said: 'But stars don't give us sunburn.'

It had been a wonderful summer, Georg, and we'd had to rub you all over with sun cream. I pulled you close to me and whispered: 'That's just because we're so very, very far away.'

As I sit writing this, you're scrabbling around on the floor building something new with your wooden train set.

This is daily life, I think. This is reality. But the door leading out of reality is open wide.

There is so much here to leave! There is so very much we leave behind.

A little while ago you came up to me and asked what I was writing on my computer. I said I was writing a letter to my very best friend.

Maybe you thought it odd that my voice sounded so sad when I said I was writing to my very best friend. 'Is it to Mummy?' you asked.

I believe I shook my head. 'Mummy is my true love,' I said. 'That's completely different.'

'What am I then?' you asked.

You'd made me fall into a trap. But I just hoisted you

on to my lap in front of the computer, hugged you and said that you were my very best friend.

Fortunately you didn't ask any more. You couldn't understand that the letter was for you. And I found it strange, too, thinking that one day you might perhaps read it.

Time, Georg. What is time?

I went on explaining, even though I knew that you couldn't understand what I was saying any more.

Space is also very old, I said, possibly fifteen billion years old. And yet no one has managed to find out how it was made. We all live in one great fairytale that nobody understands. We dance and play and chatter and laugh in a world whose origins we can't comprehend. This dancing and playing is the music of life, I said. It's found everywhere there are people, just as there's a dialling tone in every telephone.

At this you tipped your head back and looked up at me. You'd certainly grasped the bit about the dialling tone in every phone. You love picking up the phone and listening to it.

Then, Georg, I asked you a question, and it's the same question I want to ask you now, now that you're actually able to understand it. It's because of this question that I've told you the long story about the Orange Girl.

I said: 'Imagine that you were on the threshold of this fairytale, sometime billions of years ago when everything was created. And you were able to choose whether you wanted to be born to a life on this planet at some point. You wouldn't know when you were going to be born, nor how long you'd live for, but at any event it wouldn't be more than a few years. All you'd know was that, if you chose to come into the world at some point, you'd also have to leave it again one day and go away from everything. This might cause you a good deal of grief, as lots of people think that life in the great fairytale is so wonderful that the mere thought of it ending can bring tears to their eyes. Things can be so nice here that it's terribly painful to think that at some point the days will run out.'

You sat stock still on my lap. And I said: 'What would you have chosen, Georg, if there had been some higher power that gave you the choice? Perhaps we can imagine some sort of cosmic fairy in this great, strange fairytale. Would you have chosen to live a life on earth at some point, whether short or long, in a hundred thousand or a hundred million years?'

I think I sighed heavily a couple of times before going on in a harsher tone: 'Or would you have refused to join in the game because you didn't like the rules?'

You were still sitting quite still on my lap. I wonder what you were thinking. You were a living miracle. I thought your straw-coloured hair smelt of mandarin oranges. You were a living angel of flesh and blood.

You hadn't fallen asleep. But you hadn't said anything, either.

I'm certain you heard what I said; perhaps you were even listening, too. But just what was going on in your mind, I couldn't guess. We sat close. Yet suddenly there was such a chasm of distance between us.

I drew you even closer to me – maybe you thought it was so that you wouldn't feel cold. But then I let you down, Georg, for at that moment I began to cry. I hadn't intended to, and I tried to get a grip of myself right away. But I wept.

I had asked myself the same question many times during the past few weeks. Would I have elected to live a life on earth in the firm knowledge that I'd suddenly be torn away from it, and perhaps in the middle of intoxicating happiness? Or would I, even at that early stage, graciously have declined that reckless game of 'pass the parcel'? We come to this world only once. We are let into the great fairytale, only for the story to reach its end!

Well, I wasn't sure what I would have chosen. I think I would have refused to accept the conditions. If it was only for a short visit, perhaps I would politely have turned down the offer to visit the great fairytale and maybe I wouldn't even have been polite. Maybe I would have shouted back that the dilemma itself was such a load of nonsense that I wasn't going to hear any more about it. That was what I thought then, as I sat on the patio with you on my lap. I was quite sure that I would have turned down the whole thing.

If I'd chosen never to set foot inside the great fairytale, I'd never have known what I'd lost. Do you see what I'm getting at? Sometimes it's worse for us human beings to lose something dear to us than never to have had it at all. For instance, if the Orange Girl hadn't kept her promise about seeing each other every day during the six months after her return from Spain, it would have been better for me never to have met her. That's true of other fairytales, too. Do you think Cinderella would have chosen to go to the palace as its princess if she'd known she'd only be there for a week? What do you think it would have been like for her to go back after that, to her grates and pokers, to her wicked step-mother and ugly step-sisters?

But now it's your turn to answer, Georg; the floor is

yours. It was while we were both sitting out there that night under the starry sky that I made up my mind to write this long letter to you. It suddenly brought tears to my eyes. The reason I cried wasn't just because I knew I might soon be leaving you and the Orange Girl. I cried because you were so young. I cried because the two of us couldn't have a proper talk.

I ask again: what would you have chosen if you'd had the chance? Would you have elected to live a short span on earth only to be wrenched away from it all, never ever to return? Or would you have said no, thank you?

You have only these two choices. Those are the rules. In choosing to live, you also choose to die.

But Georg – promise me that you'll take time to think it over carefully before you give your answer.

Perhaps I'm going too deep now. Perhaps I'm exposing you to too much. And perhaps I have no right to do it. But your answer to the question I've posed is so very important to me, because I'm directly responsible for your being here. You could never have been in the world if I'd turned it down.

I almost feel a sense of *guilt* that I was partly responsible for bringing you into the world. In a way it was I that gave you this life, or more accurately the Orange Girl and I. But then it is we who will one day take it away from you as well. To give life to a small child is not simply to give it the great Gift of the World. It's also to take that same incomprehensible gift back.

I have to be honest with you, Georg. I say that I'd probably have said no to the offer of a lightning 'get-to-know-the-world' sightseeing tour in the great fairytale. I admit it. And if you think as I do, I feel guilty about what I have helped to set in train.

I let myself be seduced by the Orange Girl, I let myself be lured by love, I let myself be tempted by the thought of having a child. Now comes remorse and the need for reconciliation. Have I done wrong, I wonder? The question is like a cruel conflict of conscience. Then there is also the need to make good after one.

But Georg, a new dilemma can emerge here, and one that possibly isn't so difficult – or malignant – as the first one. If *you* answer that, despite everything, you would have chosen to live, even if only for a short while, then I don't really have any right to wish I hadn't been born.

So there can be a kind of balancing of accounts, one item can mitigate the other. Of course that's what I'm hoping for. Indeed, that's why I'm writing.

You can't give me a direct answer to the great question I've posed. But you can reply indirectly. You can answer in the way you choose to live this life you began when Veronika and I and a disobedient hospital doctor drank your health in champagne. That champagne doctor was a good omen for you, I'm certain of it.

Now you can lay aside this greeting from me. Now it's your turn to live.

As for me, I'm being admitted to hospital tomorrow. That was the important appointment. Mum will be taking you to nursery school from now on.

I had to write that too. And I must add: I can't promise that I'll ever return to Humleveien.

Georg! I have one final question: can I be certain that there is no life after this one? Can I be totally sure that I won't be somewhere else when you come to read this letter? No, I can't completely exclude the possibility. Because the world exists, the limits of probability have already been exceeded. Do you know what I mean by that? I'm already so full of amazement that there is a world, that I have no room for more amazement should there turn out to be another one afterwards.

I remember how, a couple of days ago, you and I killed a couple of hours with a computer game. Perhaps the game amused me more than it did you; I desperately needed a little respite from all my thoughts. But each time we 'died' in that game, a new screen immediately came up, and we were off again. How can we know that there isn't a 'new screen' for our souls as well? I don't think there is, I really don't. But the dream of something unlikely has its own special name. We call it hope.

I REMEMBERED THAT NIGHT OUT ON THE PATIO! It had penetrated my marrow, been etched on my heart. And reading about it now made the hairs on the back of my neck stand up more than once.

Until then I'd sort of forgotten everything, because I'd never have remembered that starry night if I hadn't read about it, but now I recalled it almost too vividly. PERHAPS THIS IS THE ONLY GENUINE MEMORY I HAVE OF MY FATHER.

I couldn't remember him at Fjellstølen. However hard I tried, I couldn't bring back any of the walks around Lake Sognsvann, either. But I remembered that enchanted night on the patio. That is, I remembered it in a totally different way. I remembered it like a fairytale, or like some motley-coloured dream.

I had woken up. Then Dad came in from the conservatory and lifted me high in the air. He said we were going out to fly. We were going to look at the stars, he said. We were going out to fly through space. That was why he had to dress me in warm clothes, because it was bitterly cold in space. But now Dad would show me the stars in the sky. He had to. It was the only chance we'd get, and we'd have to take it.

And I knew that my Dad was ill, too! But he didn't know that I knew. Mum had told me the secret. She'd said that Dad might have to go into hospital and that was why he was so sad. I seem to recall she'd told me that same afternoon. Maybe that was why I'd woken up; perhaps it was why I couldn't get to sleep.

Now I clearly remembered that long night of space travel with Dad on the patio. I think I'd realised that Dad might have to leave us. But first, he'd show me where he was going to.

And then – and the hairs on my neck are standing up even as I write this – as we travelled about in space, Dad suddenly began to cry. I knew why he was crying, but he didn't know that I knew. So I couldn't say anything. I just had to sit there as quiet as a mouse. What lay ahead was far too dangerous to talk about.

Then there is something else: ever since that night I've always known that the stars can't be trusted. They certainly can't save us from anything. One day we will leave the stars in the sky and go away.

When Dad and I were out sailing through space together, and he suddenly began to cry, I realised that there's nothing in the world that can be relied on.

After reading the final pages of Dad's letter, it eventually dawned on me why I'd always been so interested in space. Dad had opened my eyes to it. He was the one who'd taught me to raise my eyes from all that was humdrum down here. I'd been a little amateur astronomer long before I knew what had made me that.

And so it wasn't so odd any more that both Dad and I had been interested in the Hubble Space Telescope. I'd inherited my interest from him! I'd simply carried on where he'd left off. It was a kind of heirloom. And surely it's been like that since time immemorial. The first preparations for the Hubble Space Telescope were made in the Stone Age. Well, no, the very first preparations were made a few micro-seconds after the Big Bang when time and space were created.

There is such a thing as sowing a seed. My dad managed to do that before he died. In a way, he was the one who had given me the subject for that special assignment. I don't think Dad was much interested in football. Luckily he never saw the Spice Girls. I don't know what he thought about Roald Dahl.

I had finished reading. I'd been sitting thinking for a while when Mum knocked on the door again. 'Georg?' was all she said.

I said I'd finished the letter.

'So you'll be coming out soon?'

I said she was the one who should come in.

Then I opened the door and let her in. Fortunately she was quick to close the door behind her.

I wasn't the slightest bit embarrassed at having tears in my eyes. Mum had had tears in her eyes after her first meetings with Dad. Now I was the one who'd met him.

I put my arms round the Orange Girl's neck and said: 'Dad went away from us.'

Mum pulled me close to her. She was crying, too.

We sat on the edge of the bed for a while. Soon she began asking about what Dad had written to me. 'I'm on tenterhooks, you see,' she said. 'And in a way I'm scared as well. I'm actually a bit frightened to read it.'

I said that what my Dad had written was just one long love letter, and Mum thought I meant it was a letter of love to me. She needed to be spoon-fed. I explained that Dad had written a love letter to her, to the Orange Girl.

'I was Dad's best friend,' I said, 'but you were his true love. That's quite different.'

She sat on the bed for a long time without speaking. She was still young. After reading that long story about the Orange Girl, I could see how beautiful she was. She did look a bit like a squirrel, it was true. But just at the moment she looked more like a large nestling. I looked at her beak trembling.

'Who was my dad?' I asked.

She started. She didn't know exactly what I'd been reading all that time. She said: 'Jan Olav, of course.'

'But who was he? What was he like, I mean?'

'Ah . . .'

A hint of a Mona Lisa smile gradually formed at the corners of her mouth. She gave me an almost veiled look. I noticed now something else that my dad had observed several times. I saw how intense she was. I saw how her brown eyes flickered, or danced an uneasy dance.

'He was very, very sweet . . .' she said, 'a really rare person. And then, he was a great daydreamer, you could even say a myth-maker . . . Again and again he would say that life is a fairytale, and I really do believe that he went about with that sort of . . . almost *magical* feeling for life. He was also a great romantic . . . but then, we both were. His illness came on suddenly, and I won't try to conceal that he went to his grave with infinite sorrow. It was awful to watch, really awful. He was very fond of me . . . and of you too, of course . . . well, he adored you. And he wasn't ready to lose either of us. But he couldn't conquer the disease, either, and so he was brutally snatched away from us. He was never reconciled to his fate, not until the last. And that was why the void after him was so great . . . But there's a word I'm looking for . . .'

'I've got plenty of time.'

'He was what's called a *visionary*. That was what I was trying to say.'

Now it was my turn to smile. 'He was honest, too,' I said. 'He also had a good deal of insight into himself. He didn't even take himself too seriously. Not everyone has that quality.'

Mum sent me an uncomprehending look. 'Perhaps. But how do you know that?'

I pointed to the sheaf of papers. 'You'll be able to read it all sometime,' I said. 'Then you'll know what I mean.'

Once again the Orange Girl had to wipe her eyes. But we couldn't just sit there in my bedroom blubbing. What would Jørgen think? I didn't envy him.

'We've got to join the others,' I said.

When I emerged into the living room, I felt years older than when I'd retreated to my room with Dad's letter a few hours earlier. I felt so grown-up that I didn't mind all the curious glances that met me.

A cold meal had been set out on the large dining table. There was cold chicken, ham, Waldorf salad with orange segments and a large bowl of green salad. All five of us sat down at the table, with me at the head.

When there are lots of people present Mum often says

that 'someone will have to take charge'. That was how I felt now, and I was the one who took charge. They were all staring at me, after all. I was the main character in a way.

As we sat down to the meal I looked at all four of them and said: 'I've just read a long letter my father wrote me right before he died. And I know you're all keen to find out what he wrote . . .'

You could have heard a pin drop in the room. What was it I was trying to say? How should I go on?

'The letter was for me. But others loved my dad, too. And so I've got some good news and some bad news. I'll give you the good news first. Everyone present will get the chance to read the whole of the letter. Jørgen included. The bad news is that no one will be allowed to read it tonight.'

Grandma had been leaning expectantly across the table. Now a shadow of disappointment crossed her face. That shadow was irrefutable proof that she hadn't already read Dad's letter, not now or eleven years ago. That letter really had spent eleven years in the lining of the old push-chair.

'You must let me digest Dad's letter a bit before everyone starts talking about what he wrote,' I said. 'I also need a little time to decide how to reply to an important question he put to me. Not least, I need to find out *how* I'm to answer him.'

It was clear that everyone had accepted what I'd said. Nobody went on any more about what Dad had written. Jørgen even rose from the table and came up to me. He gave me a chummy slap on the shoulder and said: 'That sounds like a good idea, Georg. I think you're right to let it sink in a bit.'

Then I said: 'It's nearly midnight anyway. It's about time we all got some sleep.'

I could hear how grown-up and important I sounded. I was an adult now.

But I didn't sleep a wink that night. Long after the house had gone quiet I lay in bed looking out at the white landscape. It had stopped snowing hours before.

In the middle of the night I got up. I put on my down jacket, woolly hat, scarf and mittens. Then I went through the conservatory and out on to the patio. I brushed the snow off the wrought iron bench and sat down. I had turned off the porch lights.

I looked up at the sparkling night sky and tried to recapture the atmosphere of the time I'd sat here on my father's lap. I think I recall how tightly he'd held me to him. I seem to remember that was so that I wouldn't fall out of the spaceship. Then the big man with the deep voice had suddenly begun to cry.

I tried to mull over the important question he'd put to me. But I couldn't decide how to answer it.

For the first time in my life I had actually realised that I, too, would leave this world and everything I loved one day. It was a terrible thought. It was an unbearable thought. And it was Dad who'd opened my eyes to it all. That, I decided, wasn't terrible. It was great to know what lay in store. It was like knowing how much I had in the bank. And then, it was comforting to think that I was only fifteen.

And yet, perhaps it might have been better for me never to have been born, because I was already incredibly sad that one day I'd have to leave this place. But I made up my mind to do as Dad had said in his letter. I'd take plenty of time to answer the difficult question he'd posed.

I raised my head and looked up at all the stars and planets. I tried to imagine I was sitting in a spaceship. Several times I saw a shooting star. I sat like this for a long while.

After some time I heard the sound of a door. Then Mum

came out on to the patio. Dawn had only just begun to break.

'Are you sitting out here?' she asked. She could see I was.

'I couldn't sleep,' was all I said.

'Nor me,' she said.

I looked up at her. 'Put on some warm clothes, Mum, and come and sit next to me,' I said.

And soon she'd returned. She was wearing a black winter coat she'd had for as long as I could remember. Even so, I couldn't be totally sure if it was the same one she'd worn in the cathedral. But once she'd seated herself on the bench I said: 'All you need now is the big silver hair-clip.'

She clapped a hand to her mouth. 'Did he write about that?' she asked.

I replied to her question by pointing up at a large planet that had just begun to rise in the eastern sky. It was definitely a planet, because it didn't twinkle like the other stars, and I was ninety per cent sure it was Venus.

'Do you see that planet up there?' I said. 'That's Venus, but it's also known as the Morning Star. Each time Dad saw it, he thought of you.'

When the head is full of weighty thoughts, you can either say a few words, or keep silent. Mum kept silent.

After a while I said: 'I sat here the whole night with my dad before he was admitted to hospital. You can read more about it in the letter from him. But now we're the ones sitting here.'

'Georg,' Mum said, 'I'm both keen and scared to read that letter. I'd like you to be at home when I do. Will you promise that you will be?'

I touched her gently with my hand by way of promise. I thought it might be important for Mum to have me near at hand when she read Dad's letter. It wouldn't be right for

Jørgen to be the one to comfort the Orange Girl when she'd read the long letter from Jan Olav. But he could jolly well read the letter from my dad as well. He wasn't going to get off that lightly.

'It was when we were sitting here that night that Dad said he was going away from us,' I said.

She turned quickly towards me and said: 'Georg, you know . . . I don't think I can talk about this any more at the moment. It's just something you're going to have to respect. Don't you see that you're opening old wounds, too? Don't you *see* that?'

She was close to anger. She *was* angry.

'Yes, sure,' I said. 'I understand.'

After that we sat for a long time without saying much. Perhaps we were there a whole hour. I was impressed. Mum had always felt the cold badly.

I pointed up each time I saw something new in the sky, but soon the stars got fainter and fainter, and then they vanished altogether as the daylight came in.

Before we went to our beds I pointed up at the sky again and said: 'High up there is a great eye. It weighs more than eleven tons, is as large as a locomotive and moves with the aid of two long wings.'

I noticed that Mum started at this because she didn't know what I meant.

I hadn't intended to alarm her, or to tell her a ghost story. So I added quickly: 'It's the Hubble Space Telescope. It's the Eye of the Universe.'

She gave me a typical Mum-smile before reaching out with one hand in an attempt to stroke my hair. But I managed to dodge her. She still thought I was a child. Perhaps she thought I was thinking about my special assignment.

'Sometime we must find out what all this *is*,' I said.

I was allowed to stay away from school that day. Grandma said it was just a case of telling my teacher what had happened. All I needed to say was that I'd received a letter from my dad who'd died eleven years ago. When that sort of thing happens it can be good to pause for breath, she added.

When that sort of thing happens, I thought. I didn't think it was all that normal to get letters from deceased parents.

Grandma and Grandpa had to drive back to Tønsberg without reading Dad's letter. I promised them they'd be able to read it before the week was out. Grandma was a little put out about having to wait so long. After all, she was the one who'd found the letter, and she was the one who'd decided to make the trip to Oslo. But Grandpa reminded her of what Jørgen had said.

Jørgen had to go to work early that day – I only saw him briefly – but Mum and I stayed at home. Later in the morning I fell asleep on the yellow sofa as I'd not slept at all the previous night. When I awoke, we began rummaging about in the attic.

I asked Mum to dig out all her old paintings from Seville. Luckily she hadn't thrown any of them away, even though she repeated that she'd 'grown out of them'. She said this just as she was shifting her old portrait of Dad, the one that had been painted from memory. Neither of us said anything about the picture, but it took me aback when I saw it. I'd never seen such bright blue eyes in any painting before. I thought there must be a lot of cobalt in that blue pigment. And I felt that those eyes had seen something that no other human eyes ever had.

'But you haven't grown out of Dad,' I said. I didn't put it as a question. I said it more as an order.

I got her to put up her old picture of the orange trees where it used to hang, in the lobby. We took down another picture and put the old picture up exactly where it had hung when Dad had sat here writing on his computer. In the days when he had to walk carefully so as not to trip over the rails of my train layout. That was in a different time from now.

I thought that the picture of the orange trees had found its ideal position, and it wasn't too bad to look at, either. Jørgen, I thought, would just have to accept this little reversion to the way things used to be. And I said so.

We discovered my wooden train set in a large cardboard box in the attic. We found the old computer, too. I carried it down to the lobby, plugged in the screen and the computer and tried to get into the word processing programme. It was an old DOS machine, and the word processing programme was called Word Perfect. The father of one of the boys in my class still clings on to a musem piece like this, and I'd seen it started up several times.

But the programme was now asking for a code of a maximum of eight letters before opening the documents Dad had written. This was what they hadn't managed to crack eleven years ago.

Mum stood behind my chair while I busied myself with the machine. She said they'd tried all sorts of different words, and lots of numbers as well, like birthdays, car registrations and personal identity number.

I had an inkling that they hadn't used all that much imagination. Then I tapped in the seven-letter word: O-R-A-N-G-E-S. The machine went 'ping' and up came a menu that listed 'directories' on the hard disk.

139

To say that Mum was impressed is an understatement. She slapped her forehead and almost fainted.

A <dir> on old computers corresponds to 'folders' on modern machines. These, too, had names a maximum of eight letters long. One of them was called 'veronika'. I used the arrow keys and pressed ENTER. The old computers had no mouse. Only one document came up, and that was called *georg.let*. I pressed ENTER again. And hey presto, I had opened the same text that I'd read in my room on the previous evening: *Are you sitting comfortably, Georg? It's important that you're at least sitting tight, because I'm about to tell you a nailbiting story* . . . I pressed HOME, HOME and the down arrow to go through the whole document. It took for ever, at least ten seconds. And yes, the very last sentence of it was: *But the dream of something unlikely has its own special name. We call it hope.*

The really brilliant thing about finding the letter from my dad on the old computer was this. When I decided to write this book with him, I'd imagined I'd have to do a real paste and scissors editing job. But now the project would be much easier than I'd anticipated, as I could open the old document and type straight into it, before, in the middle of, and after, my dad's own text. Then I would really feel as if I was writing a book with Dad.

After a bit of messing around I got to grips with the old printer as well. It's what they called a daisy-wheel printer, and it is so unbelievable that I sometimes get into a sweat about secret agents from the Science Museum coming to steal it. It makes a noise like a chainsaw and takes four minutes to print out one page. That's because a tiny hammer has to strike every single letter against a coloured ribbon and transfer the character to paper. When my dad died eleven years ago, this equipment was well modern!

I'm sitting writing on the old machine now. And I mean now. The last thing I tapped in was: *I'm sitting writing on the old machine now. And I mean now.*

Mum has a record called *Unforgettable*. It's a totally unique recording, because in it Natalie Cole sings a duet with her father, the famous Nat 'King' Cole. Maybe this doesn't sound such a big deal, but the whole point is that Natalie Cole is singing a duet with her father almost thirty years after he died. In purely technical terms, it wasn't so difficult to do. Natalie Cole just sang over the old track of Nat 'King' Cole's recording of forty years before. You could almost say that she was moving her father's voice into a new screen.

Technically, it was no great feat to sing a duet with a man who had been dead for almost thirty years. So perhaps it was more a question of spiritual demands. But the duet is good. It's 'unforgettable'.

There is no point in eking out this story. Only two things remain. One is to answer the knotty question my dad posed. Then there is something else, too. I'll deal with the latter first, because I've decided that the very last thing in this book must be my answer to that serious question.

After messing about with old paintings and an antediluvian computer, Mum went to the kitchen to make coconut buns. She knew they were my favourite, and of course that was why she made them on that special day. But Miriam is completely mad about coconut buns, too.

When the smell of newly baked buns had begun to waft into the lobby, I went out into the kitchen. I thought I might scrounge an oven-fresh bun. And then, there was something I wanted to ask Mum about. There was a loose thread in the story about the Orange Girl. Mum hadn't read it yet.

She'd just begun to coat a couple of buns with icing. On the worktop was a bag of grated coconut which she was going to drizzle over the wet icing.

'Who was the man in the white Toyota?' I asked.

I had only asked as a joke. Really only to tease her. I already knew that he was some old flame of hers. At least, that was what she'd said to Dad.

But now she became strangely confused. First she turned to me looking pale. Then she sat down at the kitchen table.

'He wrote about *that* as well!' she sighed.

'I think he was a bit jealous,' I said.

When she didn't say anything more, I asked again: 'Can't you just tell me who was in the white Toyota?'

She gave me a thoughtful stare. It looked as if she was contemplating jumping through a plate glass window.

In a low voice she said: 'It was Jørgen.'

I felt dizzy. 'Jørgen?' I said.

She nodded. I felt even more giddy. I picked up the bag of coconut and began sprinkling it on the floor. Then I turned the bag upside down and tipped out all the contents.

'It's snowing,' I said.

Mum remained seated at the kitchen table. It was too late to stop me now anyway. All she said was: 'Why did you do that?'

'Because you're bloody daft!' I shouted. 'You had two boyfriends at once!'

She denied this strenuously. 'It wasn't like that,' she said. 'After I met Jan Olav he was the only one.'

I still felt the whole thing had been a bit fishy. 'And as soon as Jan Olav died, Jørgen was the only one?'

'No,' she said. 'It wasn't like that either. It was several years before I met Jørgen again. During those years it was just us two. You know that. But when I met Jørgen again, my fondness for him was rekindled. It took us a long time to decide to live together, a long time.'

I almost felt a bit sorry for the old chick now. She was still pale. Despite myself I said: 'Could I ask which of the two the Orange Girl was fondest of?'

'No,' she said emphatically, 'you can't ask.'

She wasn't angry, but she was firm. Then she began to cry.

I decided to let the whole matter rest, because if I'd learnt one thing from my father, it was that I had no right to meddle in things that didn't concern me. I had to be careful not to get too close to a fairytale whose rules didn't include me.

But I did have the right to think my own thoughts.

I hadn't liked what I'd heard. Because it meant that the man in the white Toyota had won in the end. It hadn't been his fault. Maybe it hadn't been anyone's fault. But I was glad my dad never knew about it.

Perhaps, in the final analysis, it was his own fault. He hadn't managed to abide by the rules. He hadn't managed to wait six months for the Orange Girl. And so it hadn't been many hours before he'd seen a dead dove in the gutter, and a white dove at that.

I will always think of my dad as a white dove. But I'm not so sure that I believe in destiny. I don't think that Dad did either. If he had, he wouldn't have been so interested in the Hubble Space Telescope.

Later in the afternoon we ate chocolate-coated buns with

Jørgen and Miriam. There were two buns with icing as well. We gave them to Jørgen and Miriam. I felt we owed it to them.

Several days after the bun-fight I'm still sitting at the old PC. I must make up my mind how to reply to the difficult question Dad put to me. I've got what I call a 'deadline' which runs out tomorrow for Sunday dinner. And then the deadline will expire.

In the past few days I've thought of practically nothing except the tricky choice I have to make. I've read the letter four times, and each time I've been left thinking: poor, poor Dad. I feel really sorry for him because he's no longer here. But the thing he was writing about didn't only apply to him. It applies to everyone all the world over, those who have come before us, those who are here now, and those who will come after us.

'We come to this world only once,' Dad wrote. Several times he said that we are only here for a short time. I'm not quite sure if my experience quite matches his. I've been here for just fifteen years, and I don't actually feel those years have been a 'short time'.

But I think I know what Dad meant. Life is short for those who are truly able to understand that one day the entire world will come to a *complete* end. Not everyone is capable of that. Not everyone has the ability to comprehend what going away for all eternity really implies. There are too many distractions, hour by hour, minute by minute, to hinder such an understanding.

Imagine that you were on the threshold of this fairytale, my dad wrote, *sometime billions of years ago when everything was created. And you were able to choose whether you wanted to be born to a life on this planet at some point. You wouldn't know when you were*

going to be born, nor how long you'd live for, but at any event it
wouldn't be more than a few years. All you'd know was that, if
you chose to come into the world at some point, you'd also have to
leave it again one day and go away from everything.

I still can't make up my mind. But I'm beginning to agree
with Dad. Maybe I'd have turned down the whole offer.
The short time I would be in the world would be so
microscopic compared to the great infinity of time both
before and afterwards.

If I knew that something tasted fantastically good, I might
still refuse a nibble if the piece I was being offered only
weighed a milligramme.

I have inherited a deep sorrow from my dad, a sorrow about
having to leave this world one day. I've learnt to think
about 'evenings like this that I'll no more be able to
know . . .'. But I've also inherited an eye for just how
fantastic life is. In the summer I'm going to do some proper
bumblebee studies. (I've got a stopwatch. It must be possible
to measure just how fast a bumblebee flies. The bee must be
weighed as well.) I wouldn't say no to a safari on the African
savannah either. I've also learnt to gaze up at the sky and
marvel at everything all those billions of light years away. I
learnt to do that before my fourth birthday.

But I can't begin right out there. I must try from another
angle. Maybe I must make this choice in my own way.

If the story of the Orange Girl had been a film, and I'd
been in a cinema watching it, in the full knowledge that I
wouldn't get a life on this planet if Jan Olav and the Orange
Girl didn't find each other – then I'd certainly have been
cheering them on, hoping that they wouldn't pass each
other by. I would have been sitting on the edge of my seat. I
would have been worried that one or other of them was

such a mega-atheist that they wouldn't have permitted themselves to take part in a Christmas service. I might have begun crying hysterically when I saw the Orange Girl suddenly turn up in the Plaza de la Alianza with a Dane! And when Veronika and Jan Olav eventually did become lovers, I'd have been petrified of the least hint of a quarrel. As far as I was concerned, a real row might have had cosmic dimensions.

The world! I would never have come here. I would never have witnessed the great mystery.

Space! I would never have looked up into a glittering starscape.

The sun! I would never have been able to place my feet on the warm sea rocks at Tønsberg. I would never have experienced a really good belly-flop.

Now I see it. Suddenly I see the full extent of it all. Only now do I understand with my life and soul the meaning of non-existence. I feel the pit of my stomach heave. I feel sick. But I feel anger as well.

I'm infuriated by the thought that one day I will vanish – and become nothing, not just for a week or two, not just for four or four hundred years, but for all time.

I feel like the victim of con trick, because first someone says: help yourself, you've got an entire world to kick your heels in. Here's your dummy, here's your train set, here's the school you'll go to in the autumn. And then, next moment there's laughter: ha, ha, we really had you there! And the whole world is wrenched away from you.

I feel betrayed by everything. There's nothing to hold on to. Nothing that can save me.

I lose not just the world, not just everyone and everything I love. I lose myself.

Hey presto – that's me gone!

I'm angry. I'm so angry I could puke at any moment. Because I've looked the Devil in the eyes. But I won't let the Devil have the last word. I turn away from the Evil One before he can get power over me. I choose life. I choose the little patch of Good that is allocated to me, and maybe there is even a being who might be called the Good One. Who can say but that there might be a God watching over everything.

I know that there is Evil because I've heard the third movement of Beethoven's Moonlight Sonata. But I also know there is Good. I know that a beautiful flower grows between the two precipices, and soon a life-loving bumblebee will take off from that flower.

Ha! I let it slip there. Fortunately there's a light-hearted *allegretto* included in this account. An amusing puppet show is playing between the two tragedies, and it's a performance I don't want to miss. I'm willing to stake everything on the second movement! There is such a thing as appetite for life, and in spite of everything I'll avoid *experiencing* the two precipices. They're not there, they don't exist, not for me. The only thing that exists is a bold *allegretto*.

I must admit, I think the thoughts I'm turning over now are pretty clever ones. It was Franz Liszt who called the second movement of the Moonlight Sonata 'a flower between two precipices'. At this moment I feel I have solved the whole dilemma.

Now I'll try going back several billion years in time. To the time when I had to decide whether to choose a life on earth in several hundreds of millions of years, or to let the chance go by because I couldn't accept the rules. But now at least I know who will be my mother and father. Now I know how *that* story began. I know a bit about who I will become fond of.

Here's the answer. I hereby make my solemn choice. I write:

Dear Dad,

Thanks for the letter you sent me. It came as a bit of a shock, and it both pleased and troubled me. But now I've finally made the difficult decision. I'm dead certain I would have chosen to live a life on earth even if only for a 'short span'. So now, at last, you can forget about all such worries. You can 'rest in peace' as people say. Thank you for hunting down that Orange Girl!

Mum is in the kitchen making dinner. She says it's going to be something French. Jørgen will soon be home from what he calls his 'Saturday jog', and Miriam is asleep. Today is 17 November and there are only five weeks left to Christmas.

You asked me some interesting questions about the Hubble Space Telescope, and the truth is that I have just written a huge special assignment on the telescope!!!

I'll tell you a big secret. I think I know what I'm getting for Christmas! Jørgen dropped some hints – at all events he showed me some really cool pictures in a newspaper and, to cut a long story short, I've got an idea that I'm getting a telescope! That would be really brilliant, but Jørgen also read that special assignment, twice in fact, even though he isn't my real Dad. He said he felt proud. I think he's as fond of me as he is of Miriam, well, almost as fond, and I don't think I've any right to ask for more. I like the guy almost as much as if he was a proper father.

If I do get a telescope for Christmas, I'll take it with me to Fjellstølen, because here in the lowlands there's too much of what astronomers call 'light pollution'. I've decided what to call my telescope. It will be christened the JAN OLAV telescope! Jørgen might find that a bit strange, but if he wants to remain on good terms with me, he'll just have to accept it.

When there's no moon, there are so many stars over Fjellstølen that you ask yourself why a space telescope was necessary. Yes, OK, Dad, I'm not really as thick as you imagine. I know that the stars in the universe don't twinkle! But sometimes it's exciting to lie on the bottom of a swimming pool for a few seconds and look up at the side of the pool. You can see something, and it's always possible to have a guess at what's happening above the surface reflection. It should at least be possible to get a good idea of the craters on the moon, the moons of Jupiter and the rings of Saturn. And then I'll just have to see if I can manage a trip in a proper space shuttle later on in life!

All my love,

Georg (who's holding the fort at Humleveien and knows he's got something really hard to live up to).

PS. After reading your letter I'll soon pluck up courage to speak to the violin girl. Perhaps even next Monday. At least now I've got some important things to talk to her about. Then perhaps, she'll show me her violin.

I call Mum. Now she's coming. As I write this sentence I'm handing her Dad's letter. She's getting the original copy.

'Now you can read the letter from Dad,' I tell her.

She can read the book I've written with him some other time, perhaps. After Christmas, anyway. And then only if I get my own telescope, because I've already woven the JAN OLAV telescope into this story.

I don't much like the thought of people reading about the violin girl. But I'm not too bothered. The idea of Mum and Jørgen reading about their snogging in the bedroom gives me the shudders, too. Well, only a bit.

Mum has taken Dad's letter and is sitting in the yellow leather sofa in the living room. She said she wanted to get in a few minutes' reading before Jørgen comes home from his Saturday jog. I've promised to stay close at hand and I can just see her through the open door. Sometimes I can hear her as well; I can hear her sniffing. I take it as a sign that she hasn't forgotten Jan Olav entirely.

But I'm still writing. That's because I've got a PS to my readers. It's just a small tip.

Ask your Mum or Dad how they met each other. Perhaps they've got an exciting story to tell. Asking both of them is better, because they may not say exactly the same thing.

You mustn't be surprised if they suddenly get a bit embarrassed; I think it's quite normal. These fairytales we're talking about are never identical, but I've begun to see that they all have rules of a more or less sensitive nature which can make them hard to talk about. Maybe you should be careful not to impinge too closely on these rules. They're not always easy to express in words, and there is such a thing as 'tact'.

I imagine that the more detailed the story is, the more

nailbiting it is to listen to because if a just a tiny detail had been different, you'd never have been born! I bet there are thousands of little things that could have made all the difference, and robbed you of the slightest chance.

Or, to borrow a few words of wisdom from my dad: life is like a huge lottery in which only the winning tickets are visible.

You who are reading this book are one of those winning tickets. Lucky you!